the secret world of

ALEX MACK ™

Junkyard Jitters!

Patricia Barnes-Svarney

A MINSTREL® BOOK

Published by POCKET BOOKS
New York   London   Toronto   Sydney   Tokyo   Singapore

A MINSTREL PAPERBACK *Original*

A Minstrel Book published by
POCKET BOOKS, a division of Simon & Schuster Inc.
1230 Avenue of the Americas, New York, NY 10020

ISBN: 0-671-00367-4

First Minstrel Books printing January 1997

10 9 8 7 6 5 4 3 2 1

Cover photography by Thomas F. Queally and Danny Feld

Printed in the U.S.A.

To Shannon, Kelly, Ben, and Kate

Junkyard Jitters!

CHAPTER 1

"Going, going . . . gone! To the gentleman with the red bow tie!" the auctioneer bellowed, slamming his gavel on the podium.

Alex Mack stood on the tips of her toes, trying to see over the shoulder of the tall woman in front of her. "Ray, I can't see what he's holding up. What is it?"

Her best friend, Raymond Alvarado, who was a little taller than Alex, peered over the woman's shoulder. "Whoa, cool! It looks like that guy just bought a magic lamp! I should have bid on that."

"A what?" Alex strained harder so she could see.

"You've heard of Aladdin's lamp," Ray said. "You know—you rub it and a genie appears and grants you five wishes."

"That's three wishes, Ray," Alex corrected.

"Oh," Ray said. "Well, then, couldn't you wish for more wishes?"

Alex rolled her eyes, then watched the man who bought the lamp walk by. "Ray," she said, glancing at the lamp, "that's a table lamp."

"Yeah, but if you squint just right, doesn't it look like a magic lamp? Sort of?"

Alex laughed and patted Ray on the shoulder. "Ray, you definitely have an overactive imagination."

"Well, you can't blame me for fantasizing about a magic lamp," Ray said. "I mean, not everyone has superpowers like you. If I had magic powers, I'd never have to wash my dad's car again, or take out the trash, or mow the lawn, or—"

"Or do so much as lift a finger," Alex finished for him. "In other words, you'd turn into a lazy blob in front of the TV."

"Yeah, but I'd be a happy blob," Ray said defensively.

Alex had to laugh at Ray; he had a way of making her do that. And that was one reason he was her closest friend. The other reason was because they shared a secret between them—the secret of her supernatural powers. Her sister was the only other person who knew. Not even her parents or her friends Robyn Russo and Nicole Wilson knew. When Alex had been doused by the GC-161, everything had changed. True, the power to morph and zap and move things with her mind made life much more simple, but it also complicated things. The people at Paradise Valley Chemical wanted to find the kid who'd been doused, to see the effects of the illegal experimental chemical. And Alex couldn't tell the truth, because if anything happened to the plant, her father could lose his job there.

Ray whistled as he glanced around the gym. "Look at all this stuff," he said. "Do you believe the *junk* people collect?" He had to speak loudly to be heard above the noise.

It was a Saturday in early January—and it was

right in the middle of Winter Break: Two whole glorious weeks of no school left. Eager to get out and enjoy the day, Alex had convinced Ray to go with her to the auction, held in Paradise Valley's junior high school gymnasium.

Alex had to agree with Raymond. It was amazing that people collected so much junk—and even more amazing that other people bought it. The entire gym looked like a giant flea market. There were rusty bikes, cracked mirrors, boxes filled with mismatched glasses and plates, old motor parts, and clothes that looked as if they belonged in a history book.

People were everywhere—sitting in the long rows of folding chairs, standing in the back, or buying food from a concession stand close to where Alex and Ray were standing. Some occasionally raised their hands to bid, while others pointed and talked about the items for sale. And above all the chatter came the voice of the auctioneer, trying to sell the objects around him.

"Actually," Alex said, giggling, "this place reminds me of your room."

"My room?" Ray asked, with a hurt look on his face.

"Yeah, your room. Like what about that old broken baseball bat you keep on the top of your bookcase?"

"Hey, that's a work of art!" he said, folding his arms across his chest. "I've had that since Little League. It took an awesome amount of strength to crack that bat down the middle. And what about your stuffed teddy bear? You know, the scruffy one with the missing eye?"

"You know very well Annie gave me that teddy bear when I won that sack race," said Alex, defending one of her favorite stuffed animals. "It's very special. In fact—hey, what's that?"

Alex leaned past Ray and stared up the aisle. One of the auction assistants was placing a box filled with old colorful hats on the auctioneer's table. There were wide-brimmed, pillbox, and sequined hats, and even a few that looked like baseball caps.

"Ray, I love those hats. Do you think I could bid on them?" she said, her eyes never leaving the box. There were some really cool hats that she could add to her collection.

As the auctioneer started the bidding at two dollars, Alex searched the front compartment of her backpack for money. She had to have a few spare bills somewhere. She winced as the auctioneer raised the price higher and higher. The box of hats was soon at four dollars.

"I know I have . . ." Alex started to say, digging deep into the pockets of her blue jeans. She pulled out two crumpled dollar bills and turned to Ray. "Do you have just a few dollars, Ray? I'll pay you back."

"Oh, no, you don't," he said, holding up his hands. "I'm not going to help add to your hat collection. Annie would kill me."

As Alex reached into her back pocket, she let out a long weary sigh. She shared a room with her older sister, Annie, and knew that one more box of stuff—hats or not—would definitely mean another boring lecture from her sister on the benefits of being neat. Alex's side of the room was filled with stacks of books and notebooks for school, CDs of her favorite groups, and of course, hats. Annie called it a disaster area, but Alex knew the exact location of everything on her side of the room, no matter how deep it was buried in a pile of stuff. *Annie's side of the room is just like her brainy, organized mind,* Alex thought, *something I'll never have—thank goodness.*

"Come on, Ray, just check, please—"

"Chill, Alex. I think I have some dollars somewhere," Ray said, reaching into his T-shirt pocket and pulling out three dollar bills.

Alex beamed. With her heart pounding and palms sweating, she raised her hand. The auctioneer saw her wave and pointed the gavel in her direction.

"We have five dollars . . . yes, five-we-got-a-five dollar, do we have a six? Anyone for six? Ah, we have a six from the lady in white! Do I hear a seven, now-a-seven?" he said, talking rapidly.

Alex frowned and reached into her jacket pocket. She had come so close—she had to find some more money somewhere. Suddenly a dollar flew out of her pocket, the bill fluttering and swirling out of Alex's grasp. She reached for the

7

flying dollar and missed. Concentrating quickly, she used her telekinetic power to send the money back to her waiting hand.

"Alex!" Ray whispered, amazed.

Alex was stunned, too. She hadn't meant to use her powers, but she needed that dollar bill. She looked around her to see if anyone had noticed what she'd done. Out of the corner of her eye, she thought she saw a small boy look at her strangely, but maybe she was just imagining it.

"Ray. Do you think anyone saw?" she said in a low voice. She leaned toward Ray and scanned the crowd in front of her. She suddenly felt mad at herself. She could have gotten herself in big trouble. Was someone watching her?

"I don't know if anyone saw," Ray said. "But you missed your chance at the hats. Look."

As Ray pointed to the auctioneer, the man's gavel slammed down on the table. "Sold! Way in the back there—the box of hats goes for seven dollars!"

Alex sighed deeply. Not only had she used her powers in public, but she had lost the box of hats as well. As an auction worker took the box to its new owner, she stood on her toes to see who'd purchased the hats. *Probably someone who has more than three dollars in her pocket*, she thought. The crowd was thick, and it was difficult to see who the other hat lover was.

As she saw hands reach out to take the box, Alex grabbed Ray's arm. "Oh, no! Look!" She turned Ray in the direction she was staring. It wasn't the hat lover who had Alex's heart thumping.

It was Vince, standing near the person with the box. . . . Vince, the head of Paradise Valley Chemical security. . . . Vince, the guy whose main purpose in life was to find the GC-161 kid and make her life miserable.

Alex panicked. What was Vince doing at the auction? Had he seen her use her powers? And if he did, would he get suspicious and come after her? She watched as Vince turned and walked slowly toward where she and Ray stood. She hunched down into the crowd around her and pulled Ray down, too.

"What are we going to do?" Alex whispered urgently. Just as Vince approached her and Ray,

9

he abruptly turned on his heel. Straightening his tie, he walked up to the front of the gym and started looking at several of the items being displayed.

As Alex let out a sigh of relief, Ray peered over the crowd to watch Vince. "He's holding up a glass jar. . . . Now he's looking over a picture frame. . . . Now he's—"

"Now he's not watching us," said Alex, pulling on Ray's arm. "Let's get out of here while he's still looking at the stuff."

Alex and Ray crouched down and moved at the pace of a racewalk, excusing themselves as they slipped past several people trying to enter the back door of the auditorium. As they reached the schoolyard, Alex smacked right into Ray, knocking her chin against his shoulder.

Peering over him, she saw the reason for his sudden stop. In the parking lot, only twenty feet away, stood a bright red Humvee—one of the chemical plant's trucks. And Dave, the driver whose truck had doused Alex with the GC-161, was at the wheel reading a newspaper!

"Just act normal," she whispered. Alex

sounded brave, but it was difficult to convince herself to stroll like a normal person and not a scared fifteen-year-old. She and Ray continued to walk casually down the sidewalk until they passed the truck, then they burst into a run. Going at full speed, they headed toward the Macks', dashing between houses, across several front lawns, down a small hill, and to the sidewalk on her street. In front of her house, she glanced behind her and saw no one was following. So she stopped and gratefully sat down on the curb. Her lungs burned, and she was totally out of breath. Huffing and puffing, Ray plopped down beside her.

Alex often wondered how long it would be before she could live the life of a normal teenager—and not always have to watch over her shoulder. No one really understood that along with the power of having super abilities came a lot of anxiety.

"Now what's wrong?" Ray said, noticing her frown. He frowned, too, and said, "We escaped Vince and Dave once again. So what gives?"

"Well, I really get sick of having to worry

about them," she answered, finally starting to breathe normally. "But that's only part of it. I guess it's about the hats, too—or, really, about not having enough money to buy the hats. I mean, Robyn always seems to have a few extra dollars in her pocket. And she had a job. Remember? She had that dog-walking service to earn extra cash."

"And she didn't really like it, especially when the dogs ate her homework," Ray responded. He scratched his head, puzzled. "So you want to walk dogs?"

"No, but I would really like to do *something* to earn extra money." Alex put her hand on her chin. "Babysitting's out. For me it seems more like bratsitting. Remember the time I watched Kelly's little sister, Jackie? She fed her spaghetti to her tropical fish."

"How can I forget."

"I really liked working for Mrs. Hardwick at the video store, but that was only for a short time. So I guess I'm all out of ideas."

"I know!" Ray said brightly, snapping his fingers. "You can help me deliver newspapers."

"Ray, I already tried that, remember? All I did was watch you miss the front porches."

"Hey, I wasn't that bad. But, listen, Alex. It wasn't like a real job back then. You just came along for the bike ride. This time, I can 'hire' you to help me."

"Ray, I don't think—"

"No, really, Alex," he said excitedly. "Not only can you deliver papers, but you can collect the money from people each week. And don't forget, I'll pay you."

"Oh, I don't know, Ray. Isn't this the paper route you're always complaining about? The one with the hills you have to pedal up and the un-friendly dogs and—"

"Well, yeah. But with someone else helping, it will be much easier—and faster," Ray insisted.

"I really don't think so, Ray. I don't want to cut into the money you earn, anyway. Maybe I should—"

"Hey, I don't mind helping you, Alex. And just think of all those tips people give you," he said, wiggling his eyebrows and nudging her with his elbow.

"Tips?"

Ray nodded.

Alex sat up straight. All of a sudden, delivering newspapers didn't sound like such a bad idea after all. Her parents would approve of her earning some extra cash. And she definitely was old enough to take on such a responsibility. Most important, if she saw something really cool that she wanted to buy, she could buy it!

"Ray, you've got yourself a deal," she said, holding out her hand.

Ray slapped five with her and said, "Believe me, Alex. You won't regret it."

CHAPTER 2

Alex dreamed she was at the auction. As the auctioneer barked out his rhythmic patter, his helper dropped a huge box in front of her. She opened it and saw it was filled to the brim with hats of every size, shape, and color. She waved her hand as the auctioneer raised the price of the hats to twenty cents—for the *whole* box! He pointed the gavel at Alex and yelled, "Sold!" Alex pulled a quarter out of her pocket, told the auctioneer to keep the change, and reached for the box. Suddenly a bell began to ring much too loudly.

But it was no bell—it was her alarm.

Alex realized she was in bed—and she wanted to stay there. She sat up, reached over, and slapped the snooze bar. Then she pulled up the covers and burrowed down under them.

"Alex," came a muffled voice.

Alex mumbled and turned over.

"Alex," came the voice again. "This is your conscience speaking."

"Sounds a lot like my sister Annie," Alex managed to say.

"Alex," Annie continued sleepily, "get up. Ray is depending on you."

Alex sat up and rubbed her eyes. "Annie, let's be real. Look out the window. It's totally dark. No one in their right mind gets up when it's totally dark."

"So who ever said you were in your right mind?"

Alex sighed and pushed back the covers. Annie was right, as usual. She had to get up, though the clock near her bed said it was not even five o'clock in the morning yet. Not only was it dark out—she was getting up early during

Winter Break! Some vacation! But she did promise Ray that she would help him with his paper route.

Alex shuffled into the bathroom, looked in the mirror, and frowned. After she washed her face, she picked up a towel and scrubbed for a few seconds. Her face turned red in response, but then it slowly returned to normal. "I look like a ghost," she muttered to no one in particular.

After brushing her teeth, she walked slowly back to her room and climbed into the first pieces of clothing she grabbed—a light blue T-shirt and jeans. After making an attempt to brush her hair, she dragged herself down the stairs to the kitchen. Alex smiled after she turned on the kitchen light. There on the table was a bowl, cereal, bread for toast—and a note that said, *"Good luck, Alex! Love, Mom."* Her mother understood what it was like to rise early to go to work: After all, Barbara Mack was once a successful account executive at a local public relations firm, who often had to rise early for meetings. Somehow, Alex realized, her mom always seemed to know how to make her feel better.

Alex poured milk on the bowl of cereal and waited for her bread to pop up from the toaster. She felt it was somehow satisfying not to have anyone around to bother her during breakfast. No one to remind her to use her napkin or say "thank you" and "please." And especially no Annie picking on her about the particular way she spread jam on her toast or slurped her cereal.

Alex jumped as someone knocked on the Macks' back door, shattering the peaceful moment. She saw Ray through the kitchen-door window and took another spoonful of cereal before getting up. As she opened the door and flicked on the back-porch light, Ray immediately handed her a grungy off-white sack filled with newspapers. He looked Alex in the eye and said, "Gee, you look like you woke up on the wrong side of the bed—twice."

"Thanks, Ray," she said, trying to polish off the rest of her toast while she held the newspaper-filled sack. "Count on you to be brutally honest."

"Don't mention it," Ray said with a shrug. "That's what friends are for." He headed outside toward his bike, while Alex laid the sack on the kitchen counter and put on her dark blue jacket. Grabbing the sack again, she checked her pocket for her key and closed the back door. As she walked up to Ray's bike, she noticed another dingy sack filled with newspapers hanging over the handlebars.

"Do you buy these sacks so dirty?" she asked.

"Didn't you ever notice how newspaper print comes off on your hands?" he said, holding up his hands. Alex squinted at them in the dim porch light.

Ray helped Alex slide the sling of the sack across her shoulders. When she felt the whole weight of the sack on her shoulder, her knees almost buckled. She didn't realize that it would be so heavy and uncomfortable to carry. She could understand why Ray used his bike, but she didn't think she was ready to throw the newspapers accurately while on her bike. "Ugh! This is heavy, Ray," she said as she tried to straighten her posture.

"Well, at least it's not raining. Then it gets heavier, or at least it feels that way," Ray said, handing Alex a flashlight. "You know, Alex, you're the only person I know of who would start work on the hardest day."

"What do you mean?" she said, struggling to move the sack to a comfortable position. She put the flashlight in her jacket pocket.

"It's Sunday, Alex," Ray said, laughing. "You're starting on the day with the heaviest paper. About five more sections than every other day."

Alex pushed the newspaper sack strap farther back on her shoulder and grimaced. "Thanks for the warning, Ray. I feel better already."

The first paper Alex threw ended up hitting a flowerpot. She started to use her powers to stop the pot from teetering back and forth when a woman in a bathrobe snapped on the porch light. The woman ran outside and grabbed the pot before it fell to the ground. "Best watch where you're throwing those papers, young lady."

"Yes, ma'am!" Alex yelled back in reply.

"Sorry! It's my first day. Umm . . . enjoy your *Paradise Valley Gazette!*" Alex shook her head as she pushed the newspaper sling farther up her shoulder for what seemed like the hundredth time. *Great*, she thought. *What a brilliant statement, Alex.*

Delivering papers at the next few houses didn't seem to get any easier. She would put her sack down, roll up the paper, and toss it gently toward the stairs. Only two of the newspapers fell on top of the stairs in front of the door. Several more landed in the middle of the yard, or fell short of the front stoop, and she had to run over to retrieve them.

At least the newspaper bag was getting lighter as she went along. Her arm was tired from all the tossing, but she wouldn't show Ray that she was hurting. After all, he didn't seem to have any trouble throwing the papers exactly where he wanted to. She gave him a thumbs-up sign, hoping he'd see it in the dim light, then turned to the next house. Rolling up the paper, she tossed it toward the front stoop. She heard a satisfying "thud"—then a loud screech.

Suddenly a small, dark patch of fur came sailing off the porch right toward her!

She ran as fast as she could, leaving her sack behind. The black ball of fur was gaining on her. She headed for Ray, who was sitting on his bike on the sidewalk—and laughing. Hoping to put the bike between her and the ball of fur, Alex ran to the other side of Ray. The animal stopped abruptly, pranced over to Ray, and began circling his legs.

"Hey, Gerty," said Ray, bending down to pick up the now-docile black cat, "what did Alex do to you?"

"Me?" said Alex, folding her arms. "That cat was after me! I didn't do anything to it!"

Gerty started to purr as Ray scratched her under the chin. "She'll chase you until she gets to know you," Ray said. "Gerty thinks she's a watchdog."

Alex let out a tired sigh. "Tell me, Ray, are there any more surprises on your newspaper route?"

"Nope."

"Good."

"Except the junkyard," Ray said.

"The junkyard?" Alex stared at Ray, not sure if she wanted to hear more.

"Yeah, the last house of the route, on Willow, a dead-end street. This guy lives there in a run-down house, and he collects all sorts of stuff. It looks kind of like the auction we went to, only worse. The old man who lives there, Mr. Bradley, yells if you don't get the paper right in front of his door."

"Gotcha. Junkyard. Paper. Right in front of his door," said Alex, watching as Ray set Gerty down on the sidewalk. The cat purred and rubbed her back against his legs. "And that's the only other surprise?" Alex inquired.

"Yup."

Alex walked back to Gerty's house to retrieve her bag. She hoisted it on her shoulder and continued on her side of the street. Maybe she should have asked Ray more questions before she started the route—and for lessons on how to throw the papers more accurately. She sighed deeply as she missed the next porch. *It's still pretty dark out*, she thought. *What if I use my pow-*

ers to get the newspapers to land on the porches? No one will know the difference, not even Ray. "Here goes!" she whispered, letting the next paper fly.

Now delivering papers became much easier. All she had to do was roll the paper, throw it toward the porch, and "help" it along with her telekinetic powers. As Alex reached her own house, she tossed the newspaper a little too far to the left. Using her powers again, she concentrated on guiding the paper toward the right. It fell gently to the porch—just as the front door opened.

Alex gasped and squinted into the dim morning light. Luckily, it was Annie at the door. But she didn't look happy.

Annie was already dressed. She strode out of the house and walked up to Alex. "Aren't you afraid someone will see you using your powers?" she asked in a low voice.

"How could you tell?"

"Believe me, I can tell. You can't hit the broad side of a barn. Remember when we used to play softball in the back yard? And when you were pitcher, you could never get the ball near home plate—"

"Okay, okay," Alex said, holding up her hand. "I get the point. But I also must bring to your attention, dear brain of the family, in case you hadn't noticed, it's not that light around here. And who in their right mind would be up this early on a Sunday?"

"Me, because your alarm woke me up," she said, crossing her arms. "Really, Alex, if I saw you use your powers, someone else may see you use them."

"Oh, all right," Alex said, groaning as she lifted up the newspaper bag. "I'll do it the hard way. I guess it doesn't matter to you if I can never use my arms again."

"No. It will make it easier for me to run experiments on you. At least you'll be still," she replied. She turned on her heel and headed back for the house.

Alex sighed. Were all big sisters so bossy and unsympathetic?

Alex felt a little better realizing that there were only about ten more houses to go. She delivered the papers by hand again, trying her best to hit the porches. At the fourth house down from the Macks', she almost hit the porch light. *I'm out of Annie's sight*, she told herself. *It won't hurt to use my powers just a little—after all, it's my first day.*

Thanks to her powers, Alex quickly reached the end of the route. As Ray had said, the last house was on Willow Street, which was a dead end. Scattered about the yard were all kinds of motors, tools, miscellaneous parts, furniture, and countless unidentifiable items. The front of the house had boards and sheets of plywood lying about, making it difficult to see the front door. Finally thinking she saw the dimly lit door in all the rubble, Alex rolled up the last newspaper from her sack and pitched it. As it sailed in a high arc, she used her powers to make it land right in front of the door. At least she thought it was in front of the door.

She walked toward the porch to check. Suddenly a huge brown dog sprung out of nowhere with a menacing growl. Panicking, Alex bolted across the front yard toward the fenced-off junkyard. The dog's mean bark scared her, and she knew he was close on her heels. Scrambling over several boards lying in her way, she felt her face starting to glow!

In the gloomy dawn light, Alex saw the outline of several large metal containers sitting just outside the junkyard gate. She jumped over a wooden box, then leaped behind the containers. Leaning against a metal drum, she tried to catch her breath. She didn't have to look at her hands to know she was glowing.

"Alex! Where are you?" she heard Ray shout.

But she couldn't answer. The dog was still after her, sniffing around a nearby path. Peeking over the container, she noticed several boxes of empty soda cans stacked in a neat pile near the fence. Alex focused on the middle box, pushing it just a little with the force of her mind. The top two boxes teetered, then fell to the ground. With a satisfying crash, the soda cans spilled all over. She breathed a sigh of relief as she saw the dog running toward the noise.

But there was another noise right behind her. Turning, Alex was suddenly looking straight into the eyes of an old man. He couldn't have been more than three or four feet away from her—close enough to see the unnatural glow of her complexion.

"Yipes!" Alex flipped up the hood of her jacket and grabbed something from her pocket. "Flashlight!" she said brightly, holding the light up to her radiant face. Without waiting for an answer, she turned, jumped back over the wooden box, and ran toward the street.

With the newspaper sack flapping at her side, she raced toward Ray. Just before she crossed the street, Alex heard a woman's voice yell out behind her.

"Bradley? What is it?"

Alex jumped on the back of Ray's bike and shouted, "We're out of here—fast!"

They sped away, and Alex made sure not to look back.

CHAPTER 3

"Alex, just calm down and tell me exactly what happened," Annie said. She put her hands on Alex's shoulders and gently pushed her down onto a bench.

After the junkyard disaster, Alex and Ray had raced back to the Macks' house. Not quite the house, but the garage, where Alex knew they would find Annie. Her parents had allowed Annie to set up a lab in the garage to work on science experiments. Unknown to them, Alex and her powers were the subject of those experiments.

Alex sat on the small bench next to some of Annie's notebooks. Ray sat beside her. "Gee," he muttered, wiping his shirtsleeve across his sweaty forehead, "I think I broke a world record of some kind back there."

Alex smiled and patted him on the shoulder. "I'd depend on you and your getaway bike any day." She took a deep breath and continued to tell Annie her story. "It was at that junkyard on Willow Street. It's on a dead-end street, the last house on Ray's newspaper route."

"And?" Annie prompted, looking down at Alex.

"And this huge dog came running out of nowhere," Alex said, shivering as she remembered. "So I ran. I hid behind a metal drum of some kind and he went right past me."

"And the old guy?"

"After the dog went by, the man was standing right behind me. I don't know how long he was there. And I was glowing, Annie," Alex said, staring at her now-normal hands. "You know what happens to me when I get scared. So I shined the flashlight in my face, hoping he'd think that's where the light was coming from."

"All right," said Annie, tapping a pencil on the desk and putting on what Alex often called her science-professor voice. "Maybe the guy didn't totally see your face. Or maybe he thought it was the flashlight that made it glow. You didn't use any of your powers in front of him, did you?"

"Well, I had to get the dog away from me, so I—"

"Alex!" said Annie, fists on her hips. "You're going to get caught if you keep trying to use your powers all the time!"

"I know, Annie, I *know*," said Alex, frustrated. "And I don't use them all the time. But in this case, it seemed like the only way to get the dog away from me."

Annie shook her head. "I think you're getting careless."

"I don't," said Ray, defending Alex. "You ever see that junkyard dog?"

Alex smiled appreciatively at her best friend. "And anyway," she continued, "it seems like it's easier for me to use my powers lately. They almost feel like a real part of me now. You know what I mean, Annie?"

Her sister stepped up to Alex. "No, Alex. I don't know what it means to be you—because I'm not you and I don't have your powers," she said, her voice becoming softer. She put her hand on Alex's shoulder. "I just want you to understand how much trouble you could get into if someone found out about your powers. Now, promise me you'll be more careful."

Alex nodded and stared at the floor.

Suddenly a horn beeped several times outside. Alex, Annie, and Ray peered out the garage door. In the driveway behind the Macks' car was a dark purple convertible, with thick chrome fenders and a small, silver horse hood ornament. Sitting in the plush, white bucket driver's seat was Niomi Mack, Alex's and Annie's great-aunt.

"Who was that, Bradley?" asked Danielle Atron, closing her leather briefcase. Ms. Atron, the chief executive officer of Paradise Valley Chemical, smoothed her white linen skirt and was about to take a seat. But she glanced at the musty sofa and thought better of it. Tony Bradley's collection of junk extended inside his house, and it was difficult to tell what was functional and what wasn't.

"Oh, just some kids outside," said Tony Bradley, pushing a box out of his way as he entered his living room. "Some young girl with a flashlight and her friend on a bike. They like to look at my junkyard. Everyone likes junk."

Vince, the head of PVC security, snorted from across the room and said, "That's a matter of opinion."

"But, Vince," Dave said, "you like to go to those junk sales." The plant's driver was standing near an old broken radio in the corner of the room, twisting knobs with no results.

"There's a big difference between an antique auction and . . . and this *stuff*," Vince said, clearing his throat and scowling at Dave. He pulled out a handkerchief and wiped his hands.

It was Mr. Bradley's turn to snort. "One person's junk is another one's treasure." He blew some dust off a rooster-shaped clock that was about three hours slow.

"That's enough, gentlemen," Danielle interrupted. She turned to Mr. Bradley and smiled sweetly. "Do you think you can do this, Bradley?"

"Well, sure," Mr. Bradley said, pulling out a drawing from his back pocket. Danielle leaned away with disgust as Bradley held up the dirty wrinkled photocopy for her to see, then laid the paper out on a nearby desk. "Shouldn't be too much of a problem for an inventor like me."

"Good," Danielle said. Clasping her briefcase to her chest, she pushed past Bradley and worked her way though the junk to the front door, trying hard not to touch anything. "I'll be back to check on your progress—or maybe I'll send Vince."

Vince rolled his eyes and said, "Yes, ma'am," with forced politeness.

Mr. Bradley ignored them and stared intently at the drawing.

"Vince?" asked Danielle, reaching for the doorknob and stopping abruptly. She eyed the knob and then gave the security guard a raised eyebrow.

"With pleasure," Vince said. He walked quickly over to the door, turned the doorknob, then wiped his hand with his handkerchief again. Looking over at Dave, who was poking through a box filled with papers, he barked, "Dave? Dave!"

"Sorry, Vince," Dave mumbled. He turned around once, as if he were mesmerized by the many objects before him. Then he moved slowly toward the door, almost as if he didn't want to leave. "This stuff is fascinating. Did you see that windup—"

"Dave," Vince said through gritted teeth, "you're driving. Remember?"

Dave's head bobbed up and down and he scurried to the door.

"Grandmack!" Mr. Mack cried out happily as he opened the driver's side of the convertible. As he and Niomi Mack hugged, Annie and Alex gathered around the car and waited for their turn.

"How are my two girls?" Grandmack said, hugging them both at the same time. "And, Ray!" She extended her hand to him. Ray smiled and grasped her hand.

"Oh, my," Barbara Mack said, coming up from behind. She hugged Grandmack and gave her a kiss. "It's another Mrs. Mack!"

Grandmack laughed at their usual joke and pushed back her sunglasses. "I hope you don't mind. I was in the neighborhood for a short visit and thought I'd stop by."

George Mack's aunt—and Alex's and Annie's great-aunt, whom they'd nicknamed "Grandmack"—"just dropped by" about twice a year. Alex didn't mind her great-aunt, though. Grandmack told wonderful stories, had cool clothes, and loved to shop, one of Alex's favorite things to do.

"Of course, you'll stay with us," said Mrs. Mack, as George reached for a suitcase in the back seat of the convertible.

"Oh, I couldn't!"

"Please, Grandmack," said Mr. Mack. "In fact,

we insist. And Annie and Alex don't mind sharing the bathroom, do you, kids?"

Alex and Annie both shrugged. "No problem," Alex said.

"So it's all settled," Barbara Mack said.

"Well, all right, then," said Grandmack, reaching into the car and pulling out three other small suitcases from under a blanket. "As long as it's only for a short time."

Alex carried one of the suitcases into the house, Annie following with another one. As they dropped the cases inside the door, Annie whispered in Alex's ear, "Be careful not to use your powers in front of Grandmack. She notices everything."

Alex rolled her eyes. "Chill, Annie. I'll be good."

It wasn't easy to get up the next morning. Alex was tired because she'd had a hard time falling asleep. She had been worrying about another encounter with the old man in the junkyard. She would have to face the house again and again—day after day. Had he seen her glowing face and would he recognize her if he saw her again? Would he tell anyone about her? Maybe she could convince Ray to switch sides of the street with her.

Moving slowly down the stairs to the kitchen, Alex felt frustrated that she couldn't use her powers to deliver papers. And her tossing arm was very sore. She sat at the kitchen table, resting her head on her good hand, and closed her eyes. No one was around, so she used her powers to fix her breakfast—tossing a slice of bread into the toaster, turning on the tea kettle for some hot water, and ripping open a package of oatmeal.

Suddenly her eyes popped open.

Turning around in her seat, Alex gasped. Grandmack stood in the doorway of the kitchen. She wore a surprised expression.

"Grandmack!" Alex exclaimed, standing up. The package of oatmeal fell and spilled on the table. Alex stood wordlessly for a second, not knowing what to do. "Grandmack," she said again. "What . . . what are you doing here? I mean, of course, you're here. I mean, what are you doing *here*? Now?"

"I always get up early."

Alex was freaked. She didn't know what to say. "Early. Yeah. Me, too, sort of." She sniffed the air and realized the room was filling with smoke. She turned to the toaster and grabbed the now-burnt toast. "Ouch!"

"Here, use the potholder." Grandmack leaned over the table and handed her the potholder.

"Thanks, Grandmack," she squeaked.

Grandmack picked up the oatmeal packet and emptied the rest of it into Alex's bowl. "I just want to know, Alex, where on earth did you learn to juggle so well?"

"Umm, school," Alex said, stammering. "No, I mean Ray. Yeah, Ray Alvarado, you know, my best friend? He was the one. He taught me how to juggle. He juggles all the time."

Grandmack smiled and nodded as she reached over and turned off the now-whistling tea kettle. Did her great aunt believe her? Alex wondered.

"He's also letting me help him with his news-paper route," Alex continued, trying to fill the uncomfortable silence. "It's really a nice route. There's even a crazy cat at one of the houses. And . . . and we go to so many houses. You wouldn't believe it."

Grandmack just smiled and nodded again. Alex was babbling and she knew it. She didn't know what else to do. Did Grandmack suspect her? Had she seen her using her powers? Alex had to admit it: Annie was right. She would definitely have to watch herself while Grandmack was in the house.

Alex jumped as someone pounded on the back door. "Ray!" she yelled, tossing the burnt piece of toast in the garbage. "Oh, Grandmack, excuse me. That's Ray. I have to get going. Can't keep the customers waiting, you know."

Alex grabbed her jacket and rushed out the door before Grandmack was able to say a word.

"Do you think she noticed?" Ray asked after she'd told him how Grandmack had been watching in the doorway as Alex made her "power breakfast."

Alex shrugged. "I can't tell, Ray. I think she thinks I was juggling."

"Annie will love to hear this," Ray said sarcastically as they headed for the first houses on their route.

"I'm not telling Annie, Ray," she said, tightly rolling up a newspaper in frustration. "I know exactly what she'd say. 'Alex Mack! How many times have I told you,'" Alex said, shaking the newspaper at Ray and mimicking her sister. "No, I'll be more careful from now on."

"Speaking of being careful, I'll take the other side of the street today. Gumbo knows me," Ray said.

"Gumbo?"

"The dog that chased you at the junkyard. It's strange," Ray said, puzzled. He removed one of the newspaper sacks from his bike. "That dog's usually pretty cool. He's never chased me before. Maybe it was your glowing face?"

"No, my face wasn't glowing until he started chasing me." She looked down at her feet. "I think I accidentally hit him with a Sunday newspaper."

"Oh. Ouch. Well, try not to hit anything with today's paper, okay?"

"No problem." Alex took the sack of newspapers from Ray and started down the street. She was determined to stop using her powers to deliver the papers. It simply wasn't worth the risk.

After twenty minutes of delivering, Alex began to get discouraged, counting her hits and misses. *That was seven missed porches and one newspaper almost on the roof of that house,* she thought, *not to mention the paper that flew apart as I tossed it.*

As she reached the last house, she looked across the street. There was a dim light on in the junkyard man's house, but no Gumbo. Ray tossed the paper on the porch, then waved at Alex. She ducked behind a telephone pole—just in case someone was watching out the window.

Ray rode over on his bike and peeked around the pole at her. "I don't think he's looking, Alex. I don't even think he's awake."

She shrugged, embarrassed. "I just want to make sure." As they walked back up the street toward home, she struggled to slip the empty newspaper sack over her head. "You really earn your money delivering papers. I didn't use my powers once today, and it was tough."

"You get used to it after a while," Ray said. He took the sack from Alex and put it into his bike basket. "But I must admit, because I deliver papers this early, I sometimes feel like a vampire. I get up before the sun rises, and I feel like sleeping during the day."

They were soon at the Macks' house, standing in the driveway. As he leaned his bike on its kickstand, Ray pulled out some bills from his pocket. "You want to come with me to drop off last week's earnings?" he asked, holding up the money. "The newspaper offices aren't too far away. And then I can give you your first two days' earnings."

"Sure. Just let me get my bike out of the garage," Alex said.

The *Paradise Valley Gazette* building was in a different neighborhood, so it took Alex and Ray about ten minutes to bike there. As they entered the red brick building, Alex was amazed at all the activity. About a dozen people were keyboarding at humming computers, printers were

43

clicking out text, and phones were ringing. Across the room, several people were standing around a desk, discussing how to fit a car advertisement into a newspaper page. Ray nudged Alex and pointed to a man at a desk in the corner of the room. With awe in his voice, he said, "That's the new editor of the newspaper."

Alex looked at the harried man standing behind the short wooden desk. His tie was loose and his shirtsleeves were rolled up. He frowned as he listened to someone on the phone. "Yes, yes, you have to remember, it's not easy to deliver papers. . . . Yes, I saw the letter to the editor complaining about not getting the paper earlier. . . . It was your letter? Well, I just want to personally apologize, Mrs. Tandy. . . . Yes, it's quite a problem. . . . Yes. . . . Mrs. Tandy . . . Mrs. Tandy? Hello? Hello?" The editor slammed the phone down.

Ray dragged a reluctant Alex to the editor's desk. "Ray, let's not bother him now," she said, pulling back.

"Mr. Decker?" Ray said, ignoring Alex and

raising his hand. "Remember me? I'm Ray Alvarado, one of your newspaper carriers."

"Oh, yes, yes, Mr. Alvarado. The one who wants to be a journalist some day."

Ray beamed. Alex grimaced, remembering how Ray was always trying out new careers. This week's was apparently journalism.

"What's up?" said Mr. Decker, shuffling some papers on his desk.

"I just want to say what a pleasure it is to work for you, sir—and the *Paradise Valley Gazette.*"

"Why, thank you, Mr. Alvarado." Mr. Decker threw several of the papers in a pile, then picked up a pen and absently put it behind his ear. "And thank you for the good job you're doing."

"Umm . . . I also wanted to ask, sir—can we help?"

Alex's head snapped toward Ray. "We?"

"Help? You want to help me, Mr. Alvarado?" Mr. Decker answered, his eyebrows lowering as he gazed at Ray.

Ray nodded. "You can call me Ray, sir."

"Ray, and—?"

"Alex, sir, Alex Mack," said Alex, holding out her hand. Mr. Decker dropped the papers and shook hands with her.

"Pleased to meet you, Alex. Maybe you two *can* help," he said, sitting down in his chair. "Can either of you come up with a better, faster way to deliver papers? That's my problem right now. I have tons of letters from people asking why they don't get their papers first thing in the morning. And people calling on the phone. They don't complain about what's in the paper—just that it's not delivered fast enough." He shook his head.

"Yes, sir," said Ray, standing up straighter. "I'll figure something out. You can count on me—us."

Alex looked at Ray and saw the glint in his eye. She knew what that meant. It meant that Ray wanted to find a way to deliver papers faster. And it also meant that, somehow, Ray would get her involved.

CHAPTER 4

Alex rolled out of bed, smiling. The sun was shining and the birds were singing. She felt wonderful. The night before, her mother and Grandmack had convinced her to take the day off from delivering newspapers. Ray didn't seem to mind—not everyone wanted the Saturday edition of the paper, so it was an easy delivery day. She had been helping Ray for about a week, being careful not to use her powers or come in contact with the old man who owned the junkyard. So she was looking forward to a visit to the mall with her mother, Annie, and Grand-mack. Her mother called it the Mack women's day off.

Alex jumped out of the car when they reached Paradise Valley Mall, almost running to the door to get inside. She finally had some money in her pocket. There were few people in the mall—it was still early—and as she went into the Clothes Closet, Alex felt as if she had the entire store to herself. She stopped at the T-shirts, spying one with a famous rock group on the front, then shook her head. She'd decided she deserved a reward for all her hard work, and that it would be something special. She continued to look around, searching through racks of brightly colored vests and white frilly blouses, not to mention way-too-expensive leather skirts. After looking at the price tag on a skirt, she returned it to the rack.

As Alex continued to walk around the rack, she heard giggling behind her. Turning, she jumped. Her friends, Robyn and Nicole, leaped out into the aisle, shouting her name.

"Gotcha, Alex. We've been following you

around the store for hours," Nicole said, laughing.

"You have not," replied Alex, laughing. "I've only been here"—she checked her watch—"less than ten minutes."

"Time flies when you're having fun," Nicole said. "So what's happening, Alex? I've been meaning to call you. Ray told me that you were helping him with his newspaper route."

"I bet you have to get up real early," said Robyn, grimacing. "But then again, it must be easier to face a bunch of quiet newspapers than a bunch of snippy little dogs." Robyn was recalling the dog-walking service she'd had a while back.

"Please don't say 'dog' to me," Alex said, a vision of the growling Gumbo popping into her head. "So what are you guys doing here?" she asked, changing the subject quickly.

"We're here with my mom to pick out a new washing machine," said Nicole. "Bor-ing! But we managed to sneak away just long enough to check out this sale."

Just then, Mrs. Wilson waved to Nicole from

outside the store. "Oh, not already," said Nicole. "I think she knows we'll buy out the whole store if she gives us over two minutes. Want to come with us, Alex?"

Alex shook her head. "Thanks anyway, Nicole. But I really think I should stay here."

"Okay. I'll give you a call," Robyn said, turning to go. "Maybe we can do something together before Winter Break is over."

Alex nodded and said goodbye. She watched as Robyn and Nicole left, then continued to browse. About an hour later, Alex was beginning to feel that every store in the mall was conspiring against her. It seemed as if they had all agreed to raise the price of everything—and those prices were just a few more dollars than Alex Mack had in her pocket. Finally she was able to find a CD on sale, one she and Ray had been talking about a few days earlier. The cashier at the store said she was one of the first people to buy the CD—it had just come in that day. Hearing that made her feel as if she had definitely found a major treasure.

As Alex left the record store to meet the others, she heard someone yell her name. It was Ray, an empty newspaper sack still hanging around his neck.

"Alex, I have to talk to you. Now," Ray said urgently. He didn't seem to notice the rest of the Mack family with her.

"Ray," Alex said, trying to remain calm so her mother and Annie wouldn't worry, "you know that CD you wanted by the Great Tune Patch? I found it!"

"Great, Alex, but—"

"And it just came in today. Do you want to see it?"

"Uh, no, not really. Alex, the dog—"

"You mean *the* dog?" Alex asked, gasping.

"Ray," said Mrs. Mack, stepping up to him, "is something wrong?"

"Oh, no, Mrs. Mack," he said, holding up his hands. "I just want to talk to Alex and Annie about . . . about—" He hesitated.

"Bicycles!" he blurted out finally.

"Computers!" Alex said at the same time.

"French class!" Annie joined in.

Mrs. Mack and Grandmack looked at each

other and shrugged. "Was I ever this confusing when I was younger?"

"Of course not, Barbara," said Grandmack. "You were more confusing."

"*Moi?*" said Mrs. Mack, her eyes opening wide in pretend shock.

Alex smiled sheepishly. "We'll just be a few minutes, Mom. Really."

"Okay," Mrs. Mack said, turning to walk with Grandmack, but watching Alex over her shoulder. "We'll meet you at the sporting shop in about ten minutes."

"Check, Mom," said Alex, making an "okay" sign with her hand. She, Annie, and Ray started walking in the opposite direction.

"You won't believe this," Ray said when they were out of earshot of Mrs. Mack and Grandmack. "I was delivering the paper near the old junkyard this morning—and not only were the old man and the dog there, but so was Danielle Atron, from the chemical plant!"

"Danielle Atron!" Alex and Annie exclaimed at the same time. Ray nodded.

"You know, I did hear someone say something

from inside the house when I ran away from the junkyard the other day. I thought that voice sounded familiar," Alex said. She stopped in her tracks. "Oh, no. Do you think the old man told Danielle Atron about the suspicious glowing kid—meaning me?"

"We can't be sure," Ray said. "I got a look through the open door, but I couldn't hear much. All I know is that Mr. Bradley was showing Ms. Atron some type of square gadget with all sorts of wires coming out of it."

"Not another gadget," said Annie, stopping and leaning against the outside wall of a shoe store. Alex knew what her sister was worried about. It seemed like every week the chemical plant people were coming up with a new gadget to find the GC-161 kid. "And don't tell me. Vince was there, too, right?" Annie said with a look of dread.

"I didn't see him," Ray replied. "But I didn't stay long. And it was still sort of dark inside the house, so I couldn't see too well. You know, that place would make a great haunted house."

Alex held her packages close. Maybe they

were worrying about nothing. Danielle Atron could have had some other business with the junkyard man. But could Alex take the chance? "Annie, I have to check this out."

"I don't agree, Alex. It may be nothing, but it also may be a trap," said Annie, shaking her head hard. "My advice is to stay away from that house. Have Ray deliver papers to Mr. Bradley from now on."

"I don't mind doing your side of the street, Alex," Ray said. "But maybe she *should* check the place out, Annie. After all, no one's better at reconnaissance missions than Alex." Ray had that gleam in his eye, which Alex recognized. He loved to go on adventures with Alex when she used her superpowers.

Annie glared at Ray. "This isn't a spy game, Ray. What if it is a chemical-company trap—and you lead your best friend right into it?"

Alex shivered.

"I know," answered Ray, "and it gives me the willies to think what they might do to her if they caught her. But with Alex's powers, Annie, I think she'd do all right."

"Yeah, you can come with us," Alex suggested.

Annie shook her head. "Count me out. I enjoy breathing." She looked at her watch. "Come on, Alex. Mom's going to be looking for us."

Alex shrugged and started following her sister toward the sporting shop. "Thanks, Ray. I'll catch you later," she said.

"Yeah, Alex. Later," Ray answered.

Alex didn't feel much like shopping after talking with Ray. Couldn't Annie see how easy it would be to check out what Mr. Bradley was up to? All she and Ray would have to do is keep him occupied. And in the meantime, Alex could easily morph, slip under the door, check out the gadget, then slip right back out.

The Mack women finally got home in the early afternoon, exhausted. Alex pushed past Annie as they walked up the stairs. Stomping into her room, she took the wrapper off her new CD and added it to her pile. She ignored Annie when she came in the room. Alex hadn't spoken to her sister since they left Ray in the mall—and she wasn't about to start.

Annie laid her new book on the nightstand, then turned to face Alex. "You're mad at me," Annie said, breaking the silence.

Alex nodded, flopping down on her bed and fussing with her CD player.

"I know, Alex," Annie said. "I'm the big bad sister. But you don't know anything about that man at the junkyard or what they might be plotting at the chemical plant. Maybe it's all innocent. Maybe the guy is working on something totally different. I just don't want you to chance it. I guess I don't want anything to happen to you."

You mean you don't want your science experiment to disappear, Alex thought. "Yeah. Right," she said out loud, staring at the cover of her new CD.

Annie sighed in frustration. She grabbed a bath towel and headed for the bathroom. As she walked out the door, Alex jumped up from her bed and followed her sister into the hallway. Focusing on the bathroom door, she pointed her finger and sent a zapper in Annie's direction—just as Annie closed the bathroom door. The zapper bounced harmlessly off the doorknob. Alex hadn't intended to hurt her sister; she just felt like using her superpowers behind her sister's back.

"Ahem."

Alex turned around slowly, her eyes wide. There stood Grandmack, her arms crossed.

"You know, Alex, I told your mother about this," Grandmack said. "And I expect she'll do something about it."

CHAPTER 5

"You . . . you told her?" Alex asked, gulping. "You mean you really told her?" *Oh, no,* she thought. *I did it again. I used my powers in front of Grandmack. And now she—and Mom—know the truth about me!*

"Yes," Grandmack said, looking down and brushing a piece of lint off her blouse. "I told Barbara there was too much static electricity in this house. I noticed it just last night. Things like lint stick right to my clothes. That's what happens when it gets too dry—static everywhere. You probably need a humidifier in here."

"Oh, yeah, right. Good idea, Grandmack," Alex managed to mumble, then backed into her room. She closed the door, fell back on her bed, and let out a sigh of relief.

"Dinner! Alex, Annie!" Mrs. Mack shouted from the kitchen.

Alex sat down next to Grandmack, and Mr. Mack sat at the end of the table. Her mother and sister sat across from Alex. She could feel an icy stare coming from her sister and avoided eye contact with her. Alex had decided not to tell Annie about Grandmack and the zapper. She knew Annie would be more than angry. Annie was mad because Alex kept bugging her all afternoon while she worked at her computer—trying to convince her sister that checking out the junkyard house would be easy. But no matter what logical reason Alex gave to Annie, her sister said she didn't think it was a good idea.

After a big bowl of spaghetti, Alex was convinced that it was a good idea. She decided to call Ray as soon as she could talk privately. Her father, who'd also finished his dinner, gave her the perfect opportunity.

"Hey, since everyone is pretty much done with dinner, I know something that Grandmack would really like," Mr. Mack said. "How about a tour of Annie's scientific workshop in the garage?"

Alex stood up. "Hey, Dad. Great idea! You should see the workshop, Grandmack. Annie's a real whiz at science. She helps me all the time with my science projects. And she has some great computer stuff out there." Alex had made her mind up about the junkyard situation, and she wanted to put her plan into action. "How about it, Grandmack. Do you want to go see Annie's 'den of science'?" she urged.

"Sure," Grandmack responded, pushing back her chair. "Sounds wonderful."

Everyone started for the back door—but Annie was the last to stand. As she walked past Alex, she scowled and said, "What are you up to now, my little cherub?"

Alex just smiled back and brought her dish to the sink. When the four Macks left the room,

Alex headed straight for the telephone. She pressed two buttons and the phone automatically dialed a number.

"Alvarado residence. Raymond Alvarado speaking."

"Ray, this is Alex," she said, whispering into the phone.

"Alex? Is that you? I can hardly hear you," came the reply.

"No one knows I'm calling you. They're all out in the garage looking over Annie's science stuff. Ray, you have to help me."

"Me? Help you? You want to bring the wrath of Annie down upon me, too?" Ray said, even before Alex could tell him what she wanted. Sometimes Alex felt like Ray knew her a little *too* well.

"Really, Ray, all you have to do is keep the junkman busy while I morph and check the place out. Easy as cake."

"Pie."

"What?"

"Easy as pie," he corrected.

"Whatever. Will you please, Ray? You're my—"

"Yeah, I know. Best friend," he said. "Come on, Al. You know I'll help you check out the junkyard. But I'll only help you on one condition."

"Just name it."

"You have to help me with my new invention to deliver newspapers."

"Sure, sure," she answered. She absently twirled the phone cord, then stopped. "Wait a minute, Ray—your what?"

"Remember how the newspaper editor was asking for a better way to deliver papers? Well, I'm going to help him. My idea is to invent a 'robot' arm that easily throws newspapers onto people's porches," he said proudly.

"Robot arm, as in the space program? Maybe you should ask space-cadet Annie, Ray."

"No, a deal is a deal. I help you; you help me. I call it my 'Flying Newspaper Deliverer'— or FND."

Alex moaned and leaned against a nearby

wall. "Ray, I'd love to help. But you know I'm not really mechanical."

"You don't have to be. Just help me solve a few problems."

"All right. It's a promise. But what problems?"

"Like how to make it work."

Alex flew down the stairs, trying to step lightly so she wouldn't wake the family up. It was early Sunday morning and she was late as usual. She didn't sleep too well that night, knowing she was going to confront the junkyard problem in the morning. But she had to find out just what was going on—and if it was something she should be worried about. Was the gadget going to be used to detect the GC-161 kid? If she could see the device, she might be able to tell.

As she swung around the stairs and into the living room, she stopped short. Lying on the floor, right in her path, was a huge white cat!

The cat opened its eyes sleepily. As Alex bent down for the animal, it looked up and let out a little screech. Jumping over a coffee table to get out of Alex's reach, it ran under the couch and stared wide-eyed at Alex.

"Here, kitty," she whispered, crawling on her hands and knees to reach under the couch. "Here, kitty, kitty." As her hand came closer, the cat ran out from under the back of the couch.

"This is ridiculous," Alex muttered. How in the world did a cat get into their house? And how was she going to get it out?

She turned to see the cat head through the kitchen doorway. It skidded across the slippery tile floor and jammed itself between the refrigerator and the wall. Alex slowly walked toward the cat, but it looked as if it would sprint at any moment. "All right, cat," she said, turning to a tall potted plant in the corner. "I'm going to have to outsmart you." She focused on the plant and, using her telekinetic power, pushed the pot toward the cat. The animal hissed—and backed up farther into its hiding spot.

Alex ran over and, hiding behind the plant, reached between the wall and refrigerator. She grabbed the squirming feline and held on.

"Sir Galahad!" someone exclaimed in a loud whisper behind her.

Grandmack was running toward Alex and the struggling cat, with her arms outstretched. "You found him!"

"Uh, yeah, I couldn't miss him," said Alex, releasing the animal to Grandmack. The cat immediately stopped squirming and started to purr.

"Oh, Sir Galahad, how many times do I have to tell you—don't wander," Grandmack whispered, holding the cat's face to her own. She then cradled the cat and said, "Thank you so much, Alex."

"You're welcome, Grandmack," said Alex, puzzled. As she rubbed the cat's back, he purred even louder. "How come I didn't see Sir Galahad before?"

"I'm hiding him, dear," Grandmack confided, leaning toward Alex. "Your father doesn't like cats."

"Oh, he likes them, but he sneezes if he gets too close."

"I know. But I couldn't keep my sweetie in

the car, could I?" Grandmack said, turning her attention back to the cat again. "You won't tell, will you, Alex?"

Alex shook her head and smiled. "No, Grandmack. I can keep a secret."

"Thanks," Grandmack said, turning and quietly carrying Sir Galahad toward the stairs. She hesitated and looked back at Alex. "I know you can keep a secret, Alex," she said. "That's another one of your hidden talents."

Hidden talents? Alex's jaw dropped. What did Grandmack mean? *Does she know about my secret powers, or . . . maybe she's talking about the juggling I told her I do.* Alex tried to calm herself down. She gave her great-aunt a smile and a wave.

Grandmack winked at her and continued up the stairs.

Alex and Ray delivered newspapers in record time. Finally they were finished—and positioned for their reconnaissance mission in front of the junkyard. Ray pushed his bike up the sidewalk, then stopped. "I'll keep him busy at the door," he whispered out of the corner of his mouth.

"You check the place out. And remember—we have a deal. I help you, and you help me come up with an invention before the end of the week."

The puddle of thick silvery liquid next to him gurgled in reply. It was Alex. She had morphed behind a bush on the side of the junkyard. All she needed was about five minutes to look around—and she was hoping Ray could keep the junkyard man busy for that long.

Ray put the bike's kickstand down and approached the porch. He bounded up the stairs, and as he knocked on the door, it creaked open slowly. Ray stepped back as he saw Gumbo's snout poke its way out the doorway.

"Back up, Gumbo, come on," Mr. Bradley said, suddenly appearing and pulling at the big dog's collar. The old man cocked his head and squinted. He looked Ray up and down. "Yes? What is it?"

"Mr. Bradley?" Ray squeaked, moving back from the dog. He held up his notepad and tried to sound businesslike. "It's me, Raymond Alvarado, your paperboy. I was wondering, did you already pay for this week's paper?"

Alex didn't hear the reply. She was already sliding slowly under the junkyard gate and making her way to the door on the side of the house. Flattening her liquid self as low as possible, she oozed under the door—and immediately came in contact with a hard object. "Ouch!" she gurgled, smacking into what looked like a wooden crate. Carefully slipping past the box, she looked around as best she could. No one was in sight. She morphed back to her human form.

Alex looked around and whistled softly. The house was a mess: junk was everywhere, piled high on tables, shelves, and along bookcases. Dozens of videotapes were stacked in the corner, right next to several broken VCR players. Magazines and newspapers were heaped on two chairs and a couch. And various sizes of pipes, poles, and plywood leaned against the walls. To get to the other side of the room, she had to climb over plastic bins and boxes filled with all sorts of nuts, bolts, and wires.

A dim light shined on a somewhat cleared-off

dark wooden table. Right in the middle of the table sat a small square gadget with red and white wires attached, similar to the one Ray described. *That has to be it*, she thought.

Alex stepped over two boxes and across a pile of newspapers to get to the table. The instrument was small, maybe as big as her fist. There were three round buttons on the front, and about five wires coming out of the side. On the table was also a piece of paper, with a drawing on it that looked similar to the gadget. Words were scribbled alongside it. "Point of view . . ." she started to read. "Central focus . . . So what does that mean?" she whispered to herself. "Maybe this is a—"

As Alex grabbed for the gadget, she heard voices. It couldn't be Ray and Mr. Bradley. They were still on the porch.

Suddenly the doorknob on the far side of the room turned. Someone was coming!

Alex panicked for a second. Closing her eyes and concentrating, she morphed, her entire body tingling as she quickly turned into a silver puddle. She moved around several boxes and pipes to get to the side-door exit, then stopped.

She didn't want to leave right away. Though she knew it was dangerous, she wanted to find out the identity of the junkman's mystery guests. As she looked back, she could see the shoes of two people enter the room.

"I don't know how anyone can live like this," said the voice of the first person. "It's so confining." Alex recognized the voice. It was Vince, the head of security from the chemical plant. And the second pair of shoes had to belong to Dave, his helper!

As they came into view, Alex froze. "I think this place is great, Vince," Dave said. He held up a long wire from a nearby table. "Who knows when you'll need a piece of wire like this. Why, the other night, one of my lamps was acting weird. I found out it was a bad wire. So, gee, Vince, if I had junk like this old wire, I could have fixed—"

"Dave," Vince said in a low menacing voice. He was so close to Dave that they were almost nose to nose. "I really don't want to hear about your petty little problems with your lamps. Got that?" As Dave nodded vigorously, Vince reached for the device on the wooden table, smiling as he looked it over. "I saw a box in the other room. I think it'll fit the thing. Now look around. See if there's anything else we can use from here."

Vince wound his way around several boxes and walked out of the room. Dave was nodding nervously, then started poking through the nearby boxes. "Oh, wow. I could have used this once," he muttered, holding up a thick piece of metal, then a small screwdriver. "And this, too."

Alex tried to stifle a laugh. Dave was talking to himself.

"Hey, what's that?" Dave asked. He leaned over a wooden crate, coming close to the side door—and Alex! She tried to keep as still as possible. In fact, she was so scared, she was hardly breathing. As Dave walked a little closer and bent down, Alex began to panic again.

"Dave!" came a voice behind him. "I told you to look around."

"Sure, Vince. I did," Dave said, turning back

toward Vince. "I didn't find much. Except we should tell Mr. Bradley about this water leak near the side door. With all this electrical equipment, it could be dangerous."

Vince picked up the gadget from the table and placed it in the small box he was carrying. "Forget about the leak," he said, smiling as he closed the box. "What do we care? We have what we came for. And I know Ms. Atron will be very pleased."

Whew! Close one, Alex thought. She heard the front door slam and realized she wasn't totally out of danger yet. Ray probably couldn't keep Mr. Bradley occupied for too long by discussing his bill. After all, Ray knew the older man had paid his newspaper fee just two days before.

Alex watched as Vince quickly handed the box to Dave and said, "Hide this under your coat."

As Vince and Dave turned to meet Mr. Bradley, Alex took the opportunity to slip out the side door. She wanted to stay longer, but she didn't want to take the chance that Dave would bring up the "water puddle" to Mr. Bradley.

She morphed back to her normal self behind

a bush just outside the junkyard fence. As she raced toward Ray, she felt frustrated. She had risked being discovered by Mr. Bradley—and Vince and Dave—but was still no further along with an answer than she had been yesterday.

At least she knew that Mr. Bradley was somehow involved with the chemical plant. And if Vince and Dave were involved, that made him even more potentially dangerous to Alex.

But why did Vince, and Danielle Atron for that matter, want that device on the table? And just what was that gadget anyway?

CHAPTER 6

"Now, if we take this piece . . ." Ray said, picking up a wire. "No, that won't work," he mumbled. He plopped down on the floor of the Macks' garage and twisted the wire around his finger.

Alex sat on a table near Ray, absorbed in her own thoughts. She knew he was trying to develop some way to deliver newspapers faster, but she was too worried about the junkyard incident to help him. Alex had to wonder if she was worrying about nothing. Maybe the chemical company had simply asked the old man for a piece of junk from his junkyard. Surely the plant had other programs going, in addition to the GC-161 project. Maybe the device was something from a junked car, truck, or even an old refrigerator. After all, she really didn't know that much about mechanical gadgets. It was even silly trying to pretend to help Ray invent his "flying newspaper deliverer."

"Sorry, Ray," she finally said. She reached for a wrench and held it up. "I guess I'm not too much of an inventor."

"Alex, I know what you're really thinking about. And if you ask me, Vince and Dave were probably just there being their usual obnoxious selves. Maybe that device isn't anything for you to worry about."

"But why was Vince so interested in it that he'd steal it? He's always trying to develop a new detector to find the GC-161 kid. That's his life's purpose."

"What about the paper you saw on the table? Did you catch the name of the device?"

"No, just a bunch of words that made no

sense. And Vince and Dave came in too soon for me to read the entire thing."

"Hey, maybe the PVC people and Mr. Bradley are friends and the old guy made the thing for Danielle Atron's birthday," he said hopefully.

Alex lifted a skeptical eyebrow and said, "Don't you think the all-important, fabulous, dressed-for-success Ms. Danielle Atron would need a pretty good reason to go to Bradley's place? I mean, I can't picture Mr. Bradley inviting her to the junkyard for cake and—"

"Junkyard? Alex, you didn't!" came a voice behind them.

Alex whirled to see her sister standing in the doorway, tapping her foot. Alex turned back to Ray and grimaced. Slowly, she stood up to face her sister. After all, she couldn't feel much worse. She might as well put up with the wrath of Annie, as Ray called it.

"Chill, Annie," said Ray, standing up. "I was with Alex. And nothing happened."

"Well, did you find anything?" Annie said.

"No. But we saw Vince and Dave, and they took some gadget from Mr. Bradley's house, without him knowing. And I didn't really get a good look at it."

Annie tapped her foot three more times, then turned to her desk.

"Annie," Alex said cautiously, "I thought you'd give me lecture number three-hundred for going to the junkyard."

"No, Alex," she said, turning on her computer. "I knew you were up to something last night when we all came out here with Grandmack. So I went inside and heard you talking with Ray. I figured it was your choice."

"Thanks," she said, almost smiling. "It was."

"So let's forget it. You've made your own decision, so you'll have to deal with it. And now I have to do some experiments on you."

"Hey," said Ray, "I was hoping Alex could help me with my invention. Now you want her all to yourself?"

"We'll share her," Annie said, opening up a notebook and clicking her pen.

"Umm, guys?" Alex asked, looking at them both. "Is anyone going to ask me?"

Ray and Annie shook their heads no in unison. Alex sighed and said, "Very funny. Ha, ha, ha."

"You know, Alex," said Ray, looking over at his bike, "we might be able to use my bike for my FND."

"FND?" Annie asked.

" 'Flying Newspaper Deliverer,' " Alex explained. "Haven't you ever heard of one of those?"

"More like Friendly but Nutty Deliverer," Annie countered, turning to her computer.

Alex chuckled. The change in conversation helped to get her mind off her problems.

"I wish we could somehow hook the pedals to the robot arm. Then as I pedaled, the arm could throw the papers." Ray turned the bike upside down and began to play with the back gears.

"Could you use a motor? Do we have one, Annie?" Alex asked.

Annie rolled her eyes. "Don't get me involved in this. You guys just keep thinking. I have to work on my science project."

Grandmack stuck her head in the garage and smiled. "Hi, guys. What's up?"

Alex held up a greasy hand. "Ray and I are trying to turn his bike into a newspaper delivering machine."

"Flying Newspaper Deliverer—or FND, please," Ray corrected. Alex and Ray proceeded to tell Grandmack all about how they wanted the FND to work, including the robot arm.

"How about hooking a motor to it?" Grandmack suggested, bending over the bike.

"That's on our list, if we can find one," Ray said, pulling off the back wheel.

"How about two robot arms to throw to both sides of the street?" Grandmack suggested.

"Umm . . . I don't know," Ray said, scratching his head. "We don't even have one robot arm working yet."

"How about using antigravity particles?"

"What?" Ray and Alex asked in unison. Annie laughed.

Grandmack chuckled and said, "Gotcha. Really, I do have an idea. I know a great guy in Paradise Valley. He's an inventor, and he doesn't live too far from here. I bet he would help you to fix up the bike. He's a whiz at this stuff. Come on. We can take my car." Grandmack strode purposefully out of the garage.

Alex, Ray, and Annie followed her to her purple convertible. Ray stuffed his bike and rear wheel into the back of the car's trunk, and they were on their way. A ride in Grandmack's convertible was always enjoyable, and Alex especially liked the stares from people as the purple car rode through the streets. Annie sat in the front with Grandmack, and Alex and Ray were in the back. The ride helped Alex almost forget about her troubles.

After about ten minutes, they rounded a curve—and Alex noticed the same store they had passed several minutes before. She leaned forward and called into the front seat, "Hey, Grandmack, do you remember where this guy lives?"

Grandmack shrugged. "I think I do, but it's been a while."

Alex and Ray exchanged glances as they rode past the Macks' house again. After riding through a few more streets, Grandmack stopped at a stop sign and looked around, then turned left. "Oh, dear. I guess I really don't remember too well. Let's see. Left, then right . . . ah, there it is," Grandmack said, pulling into the driveway of her friend's house.

Alex couldn't believe where she found herself—in Mr. Bradley's driveway. For the second time that day, she was paying a visit to the junkyard!

Annie looked back at Alex and Ray. "Is this the—" She didn't have to finish her question. The expressions that Alex and Ray wore were enough of an answer. There was no doubt that this was *the* junkyard.

"Grandmack, I was thinking," Annie suggested, talking rapidly as Grandmack turned off the car's motor. "Maybe Ray and Alex really don't need any help with their FND after all. Hey, I know—I'll help them."

"Yeah, maybe my dad has something we can use," Ray added, taking his cue from Annie. "Maybe an old noisy motorcycle motor."

Alex knew her mouth was open, but she could only nod in wordless agreement.

Grandmack opened the car door and got out. "Nonsense. Tony Bradley can do almost anything. I'm sure he'll be a great help. One time he even helped your dad invent a primitive motorized skateboard." Grandmack walked to the junkyard fence and leaned over. "Yoo-hoo! Tony Bradley!" she yelled. Gumbo came trotting over, tail wagging. Grandmack's bracelets clanged together as she patted him on the head.

Suddenly Mr. Bradley popped up from the bowels of the junkyard and waved. "Is that you, Niomi?" He walked quickly up the pathway and opened the gate with a key. Grandmack and Mr. Bradley hugged each other and laughed. Then they began catching up.

As they talked, Alex slipped down in the seat of the convertible, suddenly feeling very hot. She knew that sweat was running down her face— and probably Ray's, too. And not only that, it felt as if she was starting to glow. *Oh, not now, Alexandra*, she told herself. *Don't glow. Please, don't glow.*

She knew if she started to glow, Mr. Bradley would definitely remember her as the glowing girl—and this time, she didn't have a flashlight to get out of it.

As she tried to press farther down into the seat, Grandmack waved to the three kids again. "Annie, Alex, Ray! Come on," she called. "Mr. Bradley says he'd be glad to help us with your newspaper deliverer."

Alex looked at Annie and shook her head, as if to say, *I can't do this. Get me out of this somehow.*

"Uh, Grandmack, Alex doesn't feel well," Annie called out as Alex tried to scrunch down farther into the back seat.

"Nonsense. She was just fine two seconds ago. Come on, Tony, I'll introduce you to the gang."

Alex looked around frantically. Sitting on the floor in the back seat was a red bandanna. She quickly grabbed the cloth and wrapped it around her head.

Grandmack and Mr. Bradley walked over to the car and Grandmack made the introductions. Alex waved but kept her head down—and partially hidden with the bandanna. Ray and Annie half-heartedly said hello. Mr. Bradley winked as he pointed to Ray. "He's the one who delivers my paper with some other kid. It's sometimes late, though."

Alex gulped and pulled the bandanna down toward her eyes.

"Well, Tony, that's why we're here," Grandmack said. "The 'other kid' is my grand niece, Alex, by the way."

"Grand niece? You mean George's kid?" Mr. Bradley said.

Grandmack nodded. "Yup. Ray and Alex are the ones working on a way to deliver papers faster and better. Ray wants to rig up his bike to throw the newspapers. Think you could help, Tony?"

Mr. Bradley chuckled and pondered the idea for a moment. "Throw newspapers? Hmm," he said, stroking his chin. "You bet, Niomi. I might have just the thing. Come on inside, kids."

Ray jumped out of the car and grabbed his bike from the trunk. Peeking over the trunk lid, he watched as Grandmack and Mr. Bradley entered the house. "The coast is clear, Alex," he whispered. "They just went inside."

"You're not glowing too bright," Annie said.

"I think it's safe for us to go in. Just take a few deep breaths and try to relax."

Alex and Annie crept out of the car and walked slowly toward the house. Alex held the bandanna over her eyes, keeping her head down and watching the back of Annie's sneakers. As they walked inside and closed the door, Mr. Bradley was busy moving boxes, bags, and piles around, looking for something—and muttering to himself.

"Yup. This will work. . . . I just . . . it's right over . . . what the—" he said, shoving things out of the way, then throwing papers to the ground.

"Is something wrong, Tony?" asked Grandmack, looking up from a box of artificial flowers.

"You bet," he said, his breath coming faster. "It was right here, on this table. Someone stole my latest invention. And I think I know who."

Tony Bradley turned around slowly. He stared at Alex and Ray. The longer he stared, the hotter Alex's face grew.

Vince stood in the center of Danielle Atron's office and grinned proudly.

Danielle Atron smiled back, turning the gadget over in her hands. "So you're sure this is the device?"

"Positive, Ms. Atron," he replied. He shot a glance at Dave, who was waving to him from outside of Danielle Atron's office. Ignoring the plant driver, Vince continued, "It looks exactly like the drawing from the old files."

"Yes, Vince," she said, examining the gadget. "You're right. This is it. Does Bradley know you have it?"

"Well, not really, Ms. Atron," Vince said, smirking. "I sneaked it out in a box. That place is such a disaster area, Bradley won't know it's missing for quite some time. By then, we'll have hooked up the homing device to my latest detector—"

"And catched the GC-161 kid," Danielle finished.

"Yes, ma'am."

"And you're sure it will work?"

"I have no doubt," Vince said. "It's an old design of Bradley's from when he worked here at the chemical company. As you can see by the wires and clips, it shouldn't be difficult to attach it to my latest detector."

As Danielle took a closer look at the device, Vince continued. "My detector was never good at staying on an object. With this homing device, we can keep track of the GC-161 kid. Once it homes in on the object, it sticks to it—over hills, under bridges, through streams—anywhere. That kid will have no chance of escaping now."

Wearing a smirk, Danielle handed the device back to Vince. "If this works, Vince, we'll see about that promotion."

Vince stood up straight. "Thank you, Ms. Atron. And it *will* work."

Tony Bradley continued to scowl at Alex and Ray.

"Umm, Mr. Bradley, I . . . I mean we . . ." Alex stammered, backing up against the doorway. She reached for the doorknob, ready to bolt.

"Yup. It was the day you came to collect the newspaper money, young fellow—for the second time," he said, pointing at Ray. Alex gulped. Maybe Mr. Bradley did remember her as the glowing girl, or maybe he did see them running away from the house to escape notice by Vince and Dave.

"Yup. I left those two alone in this room," Mr. Bradley continued. "I bet they grabbed the device right then."

Alex frowned and exchanged glances with Ray. She and Ray were never in the living room together. "Us, Mr. Bradley?"

"No, no, no," he said, shaking his head. "Those two guys from the chemical plant. Said they were sent here by Ms. Atron, the head of Paradise Valley Chemical. They wanted to know if I had built something for them. Then you showed up, young fellow," he said, pointing again at Ray.

Alex blew out a deep breath and released the doorknob.

"What did they want you to build, Mr. Bradley?" Ray asked, sounding as innocent as he possibly could.

"Oh, some gizmo I invented ages ago. A homing device of some kind." As he talked, Mr. Bradley continued to throw boxes, bags, and newspapers across his living room. "It's a homing device that follows whatever it's pointed at, even if it's pointed through just about any obstacle—trees, people, boxes, buildings. Except maybe Fort Knox," he added, chuckling.

Alex, Annie, and Ray began to help pick through the junk. Grandmack stood next to Mr. Bradley and watched. But Alex knew the search was worthless. She had seen Vince and Dave take the device.

"Don't you ever tell me I have too much junk in our room, Annie," Alex whispered as she moved a box and leaned close to her sister.

Annie nodded. "For once I've got to agree with you," she said reluctantly.

"I can't believe someone stole my homing device," Mr. Bradley said, looking under a heavy box, then dropping it down. "It could only be those two goons. And blazes, I bet we could have used that device for your paper-delivery service, young fellow."

"Mr. Bradley," Alex said carefully, "do you work for the chemical plant?"

Mr. Bradley snorted. "Don't be silly," he said,

pulling out a wire from an old toaster. "I'm an inventor."

"But you worked there once," said Grandmack, helping Bradley move some newspapers.

"Sure. Years ago, I worked for the plant, when it first opened. Who didn't? And I even offered many of my inventions to the plant, but they were all turned down. Then, all of the sudden, this high-falutin' Danielle Atron shows up on my doorstep, asking me to develop one of the old inventions that I tried to give to the plant years ago."

"And you said no, right?" Grandmack asked, crossing her arms.

"Not quite, Niomi," he said, shaking his head. "It was good money, and they said it was for a new environmental process they were adding to their manufacturing plant. I didn't say yes, because it was the chemical plant, but I said I would think about it. Well, you know me, I love to tinker. So I just sat down and made the device. It took me a few days, but I finally figured it out."

"Wow," said Ray, "I wish I could do that."

Annie looked with admiration at Mr. Bradley and nodded.

Mr. Bradley beamed at Ray, then continued. "Ever since then, strange things have happened. Those two suits and a driver from the plant show up. Someone broke into my junkyard one morning and pushed over a bunch of boxes of soda cans. It took me hours to stack them up again. And some of my stuff in the living room looked like it had been moved the other day."

Alex felt awful. She knew she was the one who knocked over the cans in the junkyard *and* who moved the boxes in the living room as she searched for the device. *Poor Mr. Bradley lost his invention while Ray kept him away from Vince and Dave—just because I was so nosy*, Alex thought.

"And now the device is gone," Mr. Bradley said with a weary sigh. "I just know the two guys from the chemical plant are to blame."

Ray reached into a box and pulled out a huge wrench. "Can't you just make another one, Mr. Bradley?"

"Yeah, I guess I could. It would take another few days." He suddenly turned angry. "But, by golly, it's the principle of the thing. Why do I have to make another one? I just want the other one back. After all, it's mine."

As Mr. Bradley shifted piles of old containers filled with assorted nails, Alex leaned closer to Annie. "You know, Annie," she whispered to her sister, "I have a pretty good idea why Vince and Danielle Atron wanted this device."

Annie nodded. "Yeah. Environmental process my foot. I bet they want to home in on the GC-161 kid."

"Right," Alex said, sighing deeply. "It looks as if they haven't given up on finding me."

"So what are you going to do?" Grandmack asked Mr. Bradley, sitting down in a big leather chair.

"Call them up. Tell them off. You know, stuff like that," he replied.

"But they'll probably deny everything," Grandmack said, "and you won't get it back that way."

Tony Bradley stood in the middle of the room, his shoulders slumped. "I guess you're right," he said. "So what do we do?"

Alex moved a box out of the way and sat down on a pile of newspapers. She glanced at Ray's bike near the door, then snapped her fingers. "That's it!"

The others looked at Alex as if she had grown another head. But she didn't mind. Alex had a plan to get Mr. Bradley's invention out of the hands of Vince and Danielle Atron, and back to Mr. Bradley, where it belonged.

CHAPTER 7

"Yes, Mr. Bradley. . . . Why, of course, Mr. Bradley. . . . No, really? When? . . . Uh, huh . . . uh, huh . . . oh, could you excuse me one moment, Mr. Bradley? I have a call on my other line."

Danielle Atron pushed a button on her phone and put the caller on hold. Then she pounded on her intercom and barked, "I want Vince in here—now!"

She had hardly pushed the button to resume her call with Tony Bradley when Vince walked through the office door. Much to Vince's annoyance, Dave followed close behind.

"Yes, Mr. Bradley . . ." Ms. Atron continued, trying to smile into the phone, while at the same time glaring at Vince. "I don't know. . . . Yes, I understand. Oh, I see . . . you made the device already? . . . Oh, what a shame . . . And you didn't misplace it? . . . I hope it turns up, Mr. Bradley. Okay, yes . . . goodbye."

Danielle Atron slammed down the phone and leaned over the desk toward Vince. "In case you couldn't tell, Vince, that was Tony Bradley. Apparently, you and your accomplice here"—she waved in Dave's direction—"grabbed the device a little too soon. Tony Bradley just told me that the device was stolen—"

"Ms. Atron, please, we prefer to say we 'borrowed' it," Vince said smugly.

"And it's too bad," Danielle Atron continued, as if Vince had never said anything, "because he said the device is missing the most important part!"

Vince's eyes went wide. "What? What important part?"

"Something about a translator that fits into the back left socket—something that helps to lock on to the object you want to home in on. In other words," she said, coming from around the desk and standing in front of Vince, "something that makes the thing work!"

Vince turned to Dave. "What did you do with the device when I gave it to you, Dave? Did you drop something?"

Dave cringed, then shrugged. "No, I didn't."

"You did."

"I didn't!"

As Vince started to yell again, Ms. Atron interrupted, saying in a steely voice, "I don't care who did or didn't drop the extra part. Just get it, now. Or else."

Neither Vince nor Dave uttered a word as they ran down the stairs to the red Humvee. And neither one spoke as they traveled the streets to Tony Bradley's junkyard. As he drove, Dave would occasionally sneak a look at Vince. Vince, on the other hand, continued to fume as he looked out the window, his arms crossed.

Dave wiggled in his seat, not knowing what to say.

"I was close," Vince said, finally breaking the silence. He held his thumb and index finger an inch apart. "That close from getting that promotion. I just can't believe it."

"Maybe Mr. Bradley's lying."

Vince turned to Dave and scowled. "That's the dumbest thing I've ever heard. Face it, we could wrap that man around our little finger if we tried."

Dave shrugged. As they finally reached the junkyard, Vince shook a finger at Dave. "Follow my lead. And don't wander off."

"Do you have the device with you, Vince?" Dave whispered as they reached the rickety porch. Vince shushed him, nodded, and pointed to his vest pocket. Dave smiled and took off his hat.

Tony Bradley answered the door, holding Gumbo by the collar. He squinted at the two men. "What do you want?"

"Mr. Bradley, remember us? We're from the

chemical company," Vince said, as if he were a long-lost friend.

"Yes, I do. What do you want?" he asked gruffly as Gumbo growled.

"Ms. Atron told us how you seem to have lost the homing device we talked about before," said Vince, smiling broadly at the older man. "We're here to give our regrets. But since we're still interested in purchasing such a device from you, we thought we could at least offer our services and help you search the house."

"Well, I never thought of that. My eyes aren't what they used to be. You two are real kind," Mr. Bradley said, suddenly smiling and pulling Gumbo back. "Come on in."

Alex smiled, too, from her vantage point in the junkyard. Vince and Dave were heading into Mr. Bradley's house. *Definitely the wrong move for you two*, she thought. *But the right move to put my plan into action.* She knew that Vince and Dave were looking for the so-called missing part, not helping Mr. Bradley find the "lost device." But what the chemical-plant people didn't know was that there was no missing part. As the two plant employees walked through the door, Alex waved to Annie. Annie looked out from behind an old washing machine and signaled an "okay" with her hand.

That was the sign they agreed on so Alex could morph with no one seeing her. Alex focused her thoughts on running water, and a warm sensation ran through her body as she changed from a solid to a liquid. Slipping across the junkyard, she oozed over several old tires, a worn-out lawn chair, and a deflated football before she reached her destination—the open shed that Mr. Bradley used as a workshop.

Alex morphed back to her regular self behind the shed. Just as she hid behind a row of tall wooden boards, Vince and Dave walked down the back side steps of the house and looked around. Mr. Bradley followed, blinking in the bright sunshine. Alex peeked through the slats in the wood and watched.

"And I think it may be back here in the old shed. I thought I put the thing on my workbench. But today when I went to find it, it was gone," Mr. Bradley said. Alex was impressed with the elderly man's acting ability and had to bite her lip so she wouldn't giggle.

Vince *tsk*ed loudly. "Such a shame."

"I do most of the work out here," said the older man, pointing to the open shed. "It gets me close to all my junk. Being surrounded by all this stuff makes me feel happy while I work on an invention."

"I can imagine," said Dave, looking wistfully at the boards, pipes, and wires around him.

"Yeah—oh, I almost forgot," said Mr. Bradley, turning toward the house. "I left some water on to boil in the kitchen. You boys want some coffee?"

"Sure, Mr. Bradley," Vince replied, putting on his biggest smile. "That would be real nice."

"Good. You boys relax. I'll be right back."

Vince smiled and nodded at the old man, then turned to Dave as Mr. Bradley went back in the house. He suddenly frowned and pushed Dave toward the open shed. Taking the device out of his pocket, Vince said, "Look for something that would fit into this socket here." He turned the device over and pointed to an opening on the left. "Square, not round. All right?"

"Sure, Vince. But where do we start?"

Vince looked around the shed and pointed to a nearby workbench. "We'll start over there. You go right and I'll go left. That extra piece has to be here somewhere."

The two men searched everywhere, turning over pieces of paper, lifting boxes, and checking drawers. Alex watched through the slats as Dave pulled out drawer after drawer, smiling and looking through the contents like he was window-shopping at the mall.

Suddenly Alex had an idea. When both men's backs were turned, she focused on a box sitting on a nearby shelf. Using her telekinetic power, she concentrated on pushing the box slowly to the edge of the shelf. It teetered for a second, then crashed to the floor.

Dave jumped.

"Watch what you're doing, Dave," Vince whispered. As Dave started to protest, Vince held up his hand. "And no lip."

Dave nodded. Shaken, he continued to search.

Alex turned to another box and concentrated. The box was bigger this time and filled with small chunks of metal nuts, bolts, nails, and washers. Again she focused her thoughts on moving the box slowly across the shelf, then caused the contents to dump on the floor.

Dave jumped again. "I didn't do it!" he yelled.

Vince went over and checked the fallen box. "All this stuff is so unstable, a light breeze would knock everything down. Here," he said, handing the homing device to Dave. "Hold this while I search this box. It might be in here."

Dave nodded and took the gadget. He held it up and shook it. "Does this run on batteries, Vince?"

"Quit babbling and help me with this box," Vince said, pushing through the pieces of metal.

Alex's eyes went wide as Dave put the device down on a nearby bench so he could help Vince. The device was only a few feet away. She was so close she could just reach out and grab it—but she couldn't move from her hiding place without being discovered by Vince or Dave!

Suddenly she noticed the pile of unstable boards in front of her. Alex squatted down and leaned toward the boards. Just one little push and they fell right toward Vince and Dave.

"Look out!" Dave yelled, pushing Vince aside. Vince fell right into the seat of an old red couch, two old springs popping up on either side of him.

Dave scrambled up and grabbed Vince's arm, dragging him toward the outside of the junkyard. "Come on, Vince," he shouted, "this place is haunted!" Vince protested as Dave dragged him outside and into the junkyard. As they reached a small littered path, Vince turned toward Dave, ready to yell.

But over Dave's shoulder, Vince saw a movement toward the back of the junkyard. "Hey, you!" he yelled. He pushed Dave out of the way and headed for the person running across the yard.

Seeing that Vince and Dave were in the junkyard, Alex knew it was safe to put the next part of the plan into effect. Standing up, she reached over the workbench for the device. But it tipped and fell to the floor. Using her telekinetic powers, she concentrated on levitating the device from the floor—and right into her hand. The invention in her grasp, all she had to do was duck through the back door of the old shed and get the homing device to Mr. Bradley. Alex turned to run.

"Yipes!"

Standing in her way was Mr. Bradley. *He had seen the whole thing!* She was sure of it. "Mr. Bradley," was all she could say.

"That you, young lady? Did you get the homing device?"

"Yes, sir," she said, handing him the gadget. "Here."

Mr. Bradley grabbed the device and turned it over several times. "Well, looks like it's in one piece. Hope they didn't drop it. Come on. Let's go find Niomi and that young fellow."

Alex hesitated, puzzled that Mr. Bradley didn't say anything to her about "magically" lifting the device from the floor. She slowly followed the man out the back door of the shed.

Come on, Alex, get your act together, she thought. *Don't use your powers without checking for people around you.*

She rolled her eyes and sighed. Now she was sounding just like her sister. She hated to admit it, but Annie was right again.

CHAPTER 8

Vince and Dave scrambled through the junk-yard, trying to catch up with the running figure. "Hey, you!" Vince yelled again. "Stop, now!"

The running figure was Annie, and she had a good lead on the two chemical-plant goons. She looked back just before she charged around the side of an old automobile. Vince and Dave were still many yards away from her. Reaching into the front seat of the car, Annie pulled out a box filled with all sizes of nuts and bolts. She dumped the contents of the box on the dirt path near the car, tossed the box to the side, and hid behind a row of tall thick pipes.

Vince and Dave were heading right for her trap: As they ran around the car, they hit the dropped nuts and bolts. Arms and legs flailed, and mud flew out in all directions. Vince slipped to the left. Dave slipped to the right. They grabbed at each other—and fell with a splat into a nearby mud puddle.

"Yes!" Annie whispered, then waved to Grandmack and Ray across the junkyard.

Vince shook his arms and looked down at his suit. It was covered with mud. He grumbled and growled for close to a minute before he said anything that Dave could understand. "Give me the homing device," Vince snarled at Dave. "We're going to get to the bottom of this."

Dave sat in the mud next to Vince, trying to brush the messy muck off his arms. "It's back in the shed," he said, preoccupied with the mud.

"What?" Vince yelled.

Dave looked up with wide-eyed innocence. "You said to hold it, then you asked me to help you go through a box. So I set it down," Dave said defensively.

"You . . . you . . ." Vince started to say, then stood up, the mud dripping from his pants and jacket. He loomed in front of Dave. "I should make you go back in the shed and get it, haunted or not!"

Vince sat down wearily on the bumper of the old car and shook his head.

"Oh, young man!" came a call from across the junkyard.

Vince pulled Dave up from the mud puddle, then waved to Mr. Bradley. "We'll be right there," he yelled. As he dragged Dave toward where Tony Bradley was standing, Vince whispered, "It's time to get some answers from the old man, Dave."

Mr. Bradley suddenly ducked down behind several old refrigerators. Right next to him were Alex, Ray, and Grandmack—complete with Ray's new Flying Newspaper Deliverer and its homing device. "Sure glad you were able to grab this thing, young lady," Mr. Bradley said, putting the last wires into place on the bike's robot arm. This was the best part of their plan: To use Ray's FND idea and hook it to the homing device. Alex smiled and thought, *Luckily it won't be looking for me, the GC-161 kid—but for Vince and Dave.*

Mr. Bradley seemed to be in his glory. He smiled at Grandmack, then winked at Alex. "This contraption is perfect," he said, pushing the homing device into place. "Peek over that fridge and tell us when they get close, young lady. Then we'll see what a little ingenuity can do."

Alex peered over the appliances and saw the two mud-caked men running toward her. She ducked back down and gave Ray the thumbs-up sign.

Ray hopped on the bike, which was bolted to a frame so it wouldn't move, and began to pedal hard. As he started to huff and puff, the robot arm swung into action. It reached into the basket filled with old newspapers, grabbed a paper with its strong metal "hand," then tossed it high into the air.

"It works!" Grandmack yelled.

The thick papers flew over the refrigerator and toward Vince and Dave. But the newspaper missed its mark. "Turn on the homing device, young lady," said Mr. Bradley, holding his hand up to shade his eyes.

Alex leaned over and switched on the homing device. "Now turn it toward the targets," Mr. Bradley instructed. Alex swung the gadget toward the two men. It hummed and clicked. But the needle continued to swivel left and right, almost as if it was motioning "No."

"It doesn't seem to be working," she said, panicking and turning to Mr. Bradley.

"What? Of course it works," he said. "Stand back!" Mr. Bradley slammed a hammer into the side of the homing device. The gadget spit out sparks, then swung to the left—toward the two running chemical-plant men. As they came closer, the homing device continued to follow the two men.

"It's working!" Alex cried out.

Ray pedaled harder and Grandmack added more rolled-up newspapers to the basket. The robot arm began to work more rapidly, throwing paper after paper toward the two running men as the homing device followed their every move. One paper caught Vince in the left side and another in the leg. One opened up in midflight, showering slippery papers all over the path. The next newspaper walloped Dave in the right arm. The homing device tracked them no matter which direction they ran.

"This way," Dave yelled, grabbing Vince and heading back toward the house. As Alex watched, they turned around the corner and came to an abrupt stop. She heard snarling and growling—and knew that Gumbo was there, teeth bared and eyes staring straight at the two men. Vince and Dave backed up slowly, then broke into a run in the opposite direction.

Alex slapped Ray on the back as he stopped pedaling and wiped his brow. Grandmack and Mr. Bradley hugged each other in victory.

As Gumbo flew past their hiding place, running after Vince and Dave, Alex stopped cheering so they wouldn't hear her. Their plan was working perfectly: the two men were now running in the only direction left—out toward the gate.

"Uh, Mr. Bradley," Alex asked quickly, yelling above the celebration, "did you unlock the gate?"

"Why, no. I thought you did," he said, stopping in his tracks.

"Uh, oh." Alex turned and ran as fast as she could for the gate, hiding behind junk so the two men wouldn't see her. But they were too busy scrambling and dodging, trying to shake Gumbo off their trail. She reached the gate first and found that it was definitely locked!

She looked back. This time, she wasn't going to blow it. No one would see her use her powers. Vince and Dave were not in sight, and neither was anyone else. Alex concentrated and sent out a zapper from her fingertips. The chain around the fence shook, then dropped to the ground, fried by the electric charge sent out by her fingers.

Alex hid behind an old tractor just as Vince and Dave arrived at the gate, Gumbo loping along behind them. She watched as the two men, both still covered with drying chunks of thick mud, disappeared through the gate. She walked over to Gumbo and patted him on the head.

Without looking back, Vince and Dave peeled out in the red Humvee and headed down the street.

CHAPTER 9

"I guess we won't be seeing those two fellows for a while," Mr. Bradley said, finishing off a large slice of mushroom pizza. "We sure gave them a run for their money."

Alex pulled a string of mozzarella cheese from her pizza. Everyone was talking at once, around Mr. Bradley's kitchen table. They had fooled Vince and Dave and also got back the homing device.

"And did you see the look on Vince's face when the newspaper hit him in the leg? I could see his expression all the way across the junk-yard," Annie was saying.

"I couldn't," Ray said, wolfing down his fourth slice of pizza. "I was the one doing all the work."

"Aww . . . poor Ray," Grandmack said. She held up her glass of soda. "Well, here's to Ray for pedaling, Annie for being a decoy, and Alex for running all over!"

"And Grandmack for rolling newspapers—and, of course, Mr. Bradley for the homing device!" Annie added.

Everyone clinked their glasses together. But even though they were celebrating their victory, Alex was still uneasy. In the back of her mind, she kept thinking about how she had used her powers to pick up the device in the shed and how Mr. Bradley had seen her. Was there some reason why he didn't say anything?

"Things were a little confusing to me back there," Mr. Bradley continued, as if he could read Alex's mind. "These old eyes aren't what they used to be. I can see things on my workbench all right, but you all around this table are a big blur to me."

"So . . . so you couldn't see what was going on?" Alex asked.

"Nope. Oh, I could tell it was you from your voice," Mr. Bradley said, turning to Alex and squinting at her. "You, young lady, are always saying, 'Yipes,' whenever I'm around. Pretty jumpy, aren't you?"

"Oh, yeah," she said, exchanging glances with Annie. "I guess I do get nervous easily."

"Yes, you do. But after today you proved you are much braver than you think you are, if you ask me," said the older man.

Alex leaned back in her chair, a feeling of relief washing over her. *I can't believe it—he didn't see me,* she thought. All this time, she had been worried for nothing. Then again, if Mr. Bradley's eyesight had been better, he *could* have seen her. Annie was right. She had become awfully careless with her powers.

Ray wiggled in his seat. "Uh, Mr. Bradley?"

"Yes, young man?"

"I was thinking," he said, stroking his chin.

"That homing device sure worked well with my FND. I think it'd be a great way to deliver newspapers. Can we make a deal of some kind?"

"Deal?" the older man asked. "You want a deal? You deliver my newspapers earlier in the morning and you've got a deal."

Ray looked at Alex and smiled. "Ah, no more tossing those heavy Sunday papers, Alex."

Alex smiled back. "Sounds like a good deal to me."

Danielle Atron glared icily at her two employees and made a face. "So you both ended up being chased out of the junkyard by a large dog?" she asked, tapping her long nails on her desk.

"Well, we didn't really want to, Ms. Atron," said Vince, standing up straighter and trying to smile through a muddy face. "We think Tony Bradley rigged up his junkyard and tried to trap us . . . to get back the homing device. And we really don't think there was an extra piece. He probably lied about that. And as for the dog . . . well, the dog was pretty mean-looking."

"What about that kid, Vince?" Dave asked, scrunching up his face at Vince.

"Kid? What kid?" Danielle's voice had a sharp edge to it as she walked up to Vince. A glob of mud fell off his suit and dangerously close to Ms. Atron's shiny black shoe. She moved a few feet away from the muddied head of security.

"Uh, just some kid running through the junkyard," Vince said quickly, trying not to itch his nose with his dirty hand. "The old guy says they're always running through there."

"So let me get this straight," Danielle said, as she started to pace in front of the two men. "I send you on a simple mission. I tell you to go find the extra piece that we need for the homing device. All you have to do is find that one small piece of equipment. But you don't find it. Instead, you get chased by a kid and a dog *and* an old man—and you lose the device you originally 'borrowed,' too. Am I correct?" she asked, her words racing together at the end and her voice rising in anger.

"That . . . would . . . be . . . just about right," Vince said, hesitantly.

"Except you left out the part about falling into the mud puddle," Dave added helpfully.

Vince and Danielle turned in unison to stare at Dave.

"Just about right, eh? Wrong!" Danielle finally said, turning a withering stare back toward Vince. "I am losing my patience with both of you. One more goof-up, especially one like this, and you're both out of here."

"But . . . but . . ." Vince stuttered.

Danielle folded her arms across her chest. "Take you, your friend, and your mud out of here, Vince. And don't come back until you can think of a better story."

Vince turned and pushed the door to Danielle Atron's office wide open. Dave followed close behind. "You know, Vince," Dave said, brushing some dried mud from his pants, "it could have been worse. We could have been bitten by that dog."

Vince gave his own best withering stare to Dave and stomped away.

Mr. Decker was standing on the front steps of the newspaper building. He motioned for Ray to begin his bike ride. "We'll see how this goes, Max," he said to the managing editor next to him. "What did he call this thing?"

"A Flying Newspaper Deliverer, sir," Alex answered, standing on the other side of the editor. "He also calls it his FND."

The editor laughed. "And what is your job in all this?"

"We take turns. Sometimes I keep the paper supply going, sometimes Ray does," Alex explained, shading her eyes with her hands and watching her best friend start his ride. "Sometimes I ride, sometimes Ray does. It's sort of a joint effort, Mr. Decker."

She watched as the robot arm grabbed a newspaper. As the bike came closer, Ray hit a switch. The arm threw the newspaper—and it fell right at Mr. Decker's feet.

Max cheered as Ray rode by. Mr. Decker raised his hands and clapped. "All right, Ray—this is a great machine! I wish we could afford to buy a bunch of them for all the other newspaper carriers."

Ray turned the bike around and headed back

toward Mr. Decker. Ray had a big smile on his face, and Alex knew just what it meant: he was smiling at the prospect of making tons of money. "Well, Mr. Decker," he said, turning off the homing device, "all it takes is a bike and Mr. Bradley."

"Ah, yes, the junkyard man. He was a great inventor once," the editor said.

"He still is, sir," came the reply from Ray. He pointed to a man standing across the parking lot. "He's way over there on the other side."

Mr. Decker waved to Mr. Bradley. The older man, now wearing glasses, waved back. "Who's the woman?"

"That's my great-aunt," Alex responded, waving to them. "She's a friend of Mr. Bradley's, too."

Mr. Decker cleared his throat and turned to Alex and Ray. "You two have done a great job, especially for your paper route," he said. He took a clipboard and pen from the managing editor. "Max? I think these two deserve not only a bonus for their invention—but they also deserve a write-up in the paper."

"Us?" said Alex and Ray in unison.

"That's right. I'll even write the article myself," said Mr. Decker, jotting something down on the clipboard. He tore off part of the paper and handed it to Alex. "Here. Meet me back at the newspaper building next Tuesday at this time. We'll do the interview then. And don't forget the bike. We'll get pictures."

Ray looked back across the parking lot. "And Mr. Bradley?"

Mr. Decker smiled. "Yes, by all means, bring him along, too."

Alex and Ray ran toward Mr. Bradley and Grandmack. Alex tried to slow down her explanation of what happened, but she knew she was talking too fast. She didn't really care—she was so excited.

"Us!" she said with awe. "Us in the papers—wow!"

"And the bonus," Ray added. "Maybe I can buy that yacht I've always wanted."

Alex slapped him lightly in the arm. "Ray, don't you remember?" She turned to the older man and said, "We want to split the bonus money with you. After all, you were the one who invented the homing device."

Mr. Bradley shook his head. "No way, young lady. You and your friend keep the bonus. It's enough you two helped me get back my homing device from those rascals. Plus, Gumbo and I haven't had such an adventure in a long time!"

CHAPTER 10

Alex shuffled into the garage and dropped down into a chair next to Annie. Her sister was sitting at her desk, intent on something she was typing into her laptop computer. Picking up one of Annie's science notebooks, Alex idly turned the pages.

"Since when did you become a mad scientist?" asked her sister, without looking away from her computer screen.

"I'm not interested in your notebooks," she said, sighing. "It's just, you know, something to do."

It was a few days after she and Ray had shown off their delivery bike to the editor of the *Paradise Valley Gazette*. Both of them received a big bonus of fifty dollars each—and to celebrate, George Mack took the family and Ray out to dinner at Alex's favorite Italian restaurant. Alex already knew how she wanted to spend the money. She had her sights set on a leather skirt. Even the article about Alex and Ray was coming out soon. Everything seemed just right with the world.

But Alex felt simply awful.

For several years, Annie had written down detailed records about Alex's powers. She had carefully noted any problems that Alex encountered. She took such pains out of concern for her sister and the effects of GC-161 on her. And in a way, as Alex looked back, it was a wonderful chance to get closer to Annie.

And now, she thought, *I may have destroyed it all—just by being dumb about when or when not to use my powers.*

"I can't believe she doesn't know, Alex," said Annie, leaning back in her chair and clasping her hands behind her head. "If you're right and

Grandmack was behind you all those times, she must be aware of your powers."

"I know." Alex put the notebook down on the desk. "And she said something about my hidden talents. What do we do, Annie. Do we tell her?"

Annie turned and looked into Alex's eyes. "I think it should be your call, Alex."

Alex leaned forward on the desk and rested her head in her arms. Ever since the accident, she had wished she could tell an adult about her special powers. Maybe then, life would be easier. She thought by telling her mother and father about her secret that she could somehow use her powers to help others—especially her friends and family. But in reality, Alex knew what revealing her powers would mean. It would mean that everyone would fear for her safety. It would mean that she would be looked upon as a freak. Some people would even be afraid of her and her powers. And it also could mean she'd be closed up in a room forever, subjected to test after test by Danielle Atron and Vince.

"Maybe we can tell Grandmack—and then

convince her to keep it a secret," Alex finally said.

Annie shook her head. "Yeah, but for how long? And would she keep it a secret, especially if she thought you were in danger?"

Alex looked up at her sister. "But I'm not in danger, Annie. At least not for now," she answered, putting her head back on her arms.

"Alex! Annie!" Grandmack's voice rang through the garage. Suddenly she appeared at the garage door. "Hey, you two! I'm leaving now. I just wanted to thank you for shopping, sharing the bathroom with me—and for a wonderful adventure! I feel like a new woman."

Alex stood up slowly and took a deep breath. As she turned to Grandmack, Annie grabbed her sister's hand. Alex shook her head. "No, Annie. I think I should do this."

Alex squared her shoulders and moved in front of Grandmack. "Grandmack," she said clearly, her stomach churning. "We . . . I have something to tell you." She took a deep breath, then let it out. "I want you to know . . . all those things you saw . . . Grandmack, I have special powers."

Grandmack smiled. "I know."

Alex's heart sunk to her feet. It was true. She *had* seen all those things Alex had done in front of her. Grandmack knew she had powers. "Well, I can explain, really, Grandmack—"

Grandmack held up her hand. "That's not necessary, Alex. Now I'm not saying you don't have special powers, too, Annie," she said, turning toward Annie. "You are wonderful in the sciences and mathematics. And I'm very proud of you." She turned back to Alex. "But Alex? She's very special, too. Why, I can't tell you how many things she does and does well. I saw her juggling in the kitchen once. And she has a wonderful way with animals—don't you, Alex?" she added, winking. "Then she popped that chain off the fence at Bradley's place to let Vince and Dave out the gate. Would you ever think she was that strong? And she runs fast, too. I could hardly keep up with her!"

"But—" Alex started.

"I think, Alexandra Mack, that you have the

special powers to do anything you want to. That's all I need to know," Grandmack said. She brushed a lock of hair from Alex's forehead. "You're really something."

Alex and Annie looked at each other and smiled. "Yeah," Annie said, still looking at her sister, "she's something all right."

Alex hugged Annie, then they both hugged Grandmack.

It was a warm springlike day, and as Grandmack revved the motor of her convertible, she pushed the button that brought the top down. Suddenly she put her hand to her forehead. "Oh, Alex!" she called, turning to look at Alex, her bracelets clanging as she spun around. "Would you be a dear and go get a box I forgot on your bed?"

"Sure," Alex said, running back into the house. Leaping up the stairs two by two, she made it to her room in record time.

There, on the bed, was a medium-size box filled with hats. And not just any hats—but the hats from the auction she and Ray had attended at the school gymnasium. Alex reached for the pillbox hat lying on top and put it on her head. Beaming with unexpected pleasure, she looked in the mirror. A note fluttered to the ground, and she picked it up. "For my talented grand-niece, Alex," she said, reading the note out loud, "who has the power to do anything she wants."

Oh, my gosh—Grandmack was at the auction, she thought. *I wonder if she saw . . .*

Alex heard a car accelerating out front. She grabbed a floppy-brimmed hat and flew down the stairs. Everyone had gone inside and Grand-mack was driving away in her convertible, Sir Galahad popping up from under a blanket and snuggling by her side.

"Grandmack! Wait!" Alex called to her.

Grandmack stopped the car and Sir Galahad stood with his paws on the passenger-side door, looking back. As Grandmack watched, Alex tossed the floppy hat. It sailed toward Grand-mack, but it was flying a little too much to the left. Using her telekinetic powers, Alex concen-trated and sent the hat to its destination. The hat fell right on top of Grandmack's head.

Grandmack looked amazed, then smiled. Alex knew that look—a look that said Grandmack would always be amazed at Alex's talents—and "special powers." Alex waved as they sped off, with a honk of the horn from Grandmack and a meow from Sir Galahad.

About the Author

PATRICIA BARNES-SVARNEY has as many stuffed animals as Alex Mack has hats—and she's proud of it. She writes not only fiction but also nonfiction, and you can often see her name lurking in science magazine articles and along the bindings of books for young readers and adults. When she's not writing, she likes to spend her time reading, birding, herb gardening, and hiking. She is the author of *Stark Trek: The Next Generation: Starfleet Academy: Loyalties*, a novel for young readers. She is working on another story about *The Secret World of Alex Mack* and *Star Trek*. She lives with her husband in Endwell, New York.